THE CLEARING

OTHER BOOKS BY ALAN ARKIN

THE
CLEARING

Alan Arkin

1817

Harper & Row, Publishers, San Francisco
Cambridge, Hagerstown, New York, Philadelphia
London, Mexico City, São Paulo, Singapore, Sydney

FIRST EDITION

Designed by Donald Hatch

Library of Congress Cataloging-in-Publication Data

Arkin, Alan.
  The clearing.

  Summary: Bubber the Lemming joins a group of forest
animals in their quest for spiritual understanding
and self-knowledge.
  [1. Lemmings—Fiction. 2. Animals—Fiction.
3. Self-perception—Fiction] I. Title.
PZ7.A687C 1986   [Fic]   85-45345
ISBN 0-06-250032-5
ISBN 0-06-020140-1 (lib. bdg.)

---

86 87 88 89 90 HC 10 9 8 7 6 5 4 3 2 1

To Sanyama and the Lions of Hari

CHAPTER 1

Cougar had been summoned by the bear, and the news made him so happy that he almost wept for joy. For weeks now, Cougar had been banished from the clearing, and he had begun to fear that this time it would be forever. But being summoned could only mean that he was back in the bear's good graces, and perhaps that he was even needed for something. Cougar fervently hoped that he was needed, and if so that it was for something enormous and important, so that he could prove to the bear once and for all how much he had changed, how reliable and steady he had become. He set out for the clearing immediately, and when he arrived he found the bear sitting completely still and gazing off into the middle distance. Cougar had seen the bear in this state many times before, but it always made him uncomfortable. He padded around for a while, pretending to be quiet, coughing occasionally and yawning loudly, but the noise didn't have the desired effect. He sat down and tried to do a "hum" to pass the time, but just as he started, the bear spoke.

"Find the lemon," said the Bear, in an odd and distant tone. "He'll be headed in our direction."

"Lemons don't head anywhere," Cougar told him politely but firmly, "They are a fruit. They have no means of locomotion."

Bear sighed his weary sigh, which always infuriated Cougar, looked heavenward, and began shambling off toward his cave.

"How will I know him when I see him?" Cougar

- 1 -

called out, and then realized what a stupid question that was. There would be no way to miss a walking lemon. "Where is he coming from, then?" called Cougar.

"From the west," said the bear over his shoulder without looking back.

"The west?" Cougar shouted incredulously. "From the west? That's a pretty big area. It covers one quarter of everything. Could you be a little more specific?"

By this time the bear had gone back into his cave and the conversation was over. Cougar waited outside in the hopes that Bear would come out again with more information, but before long Bear's loud "hum" could be heard from deep inside the cave and that meant Bear would be occupied for hours, maybe days. Cougar stared at the mouth of the cave for a moment, then abruptly turned. "Right," he said. "Find the lemon in the west. Find the walking lemon in the west." The search was going to be impossible, not only because of what he had to look for, and the area that he had to cover, but because there would be no one to help him. His nature was so unpredictable that hardly a creature in the forest would have anything to do with him. Usually this gave him a sense of superiority, but on this occasion he realized it would be a bit of a disadvantage. Once in a while he could get a hello from a skunk, a nod from a badger, but since their life's work was to know nothing about anything they would be of no help whatever. "Well," he sighed; he had wanted a challenge, and here it was.

Cougar headed away from the clearing with great determination and for almost two full days made a valiant effort to find what he had been sent for, but in the middle of the second afternoon his enthusiasm began to wane. Anger started to well up inside him in great spasms and no matter how many "hums" he did the anger wouldn't go away. What's more, he was beginning to enjoy the anger's company, and he began to think lovingly about screaming at the top of his lungs and clawing down some trees. There were no lemons in this part of the world. Cougar knew that with absolute certainty. They grew in warm climates, and the only movement they were capable of was falling off trees, and why he had been out searching for one was absolutely beyond him. What's more, for the bear to have even asked such a thing from him meant that Bear had finally gone crazy. It was a suspicion that had crossed Cougar's mind many times in the past, but this insane mission was the final confirmation. He had been made a fool of by a deranged bear. It was the last straw. Because of his own childlike and sensitive nature, he had mistaken madness for wisdom. Well, it would not happen again. Bear could find another flunky to run his errands. By this time Cougar had wandered into the high country and to calm himself down he walked over to a huge rock promontory and stood there, looking out suspiciously over most of the western world. But the view had no soothing effect on him. What would happen if he ran into Bear on the way home? he thought to himself, Or one of the other animals from the clearing? What if they had sent him on this mission as a joke? Or in order to get rid of him? Well, he might just have to knock them around a little and show them what was serious in the world, and also to teach them something about wasting other folks' time. Cougar quickly turned away from the rocks and with his head held high he strode purposefully back toward home, and before long he had regained enough bluster and swagger to carry him through any chance encounter he might have with Bear or one of his stooges. To pump himself up even further, he began working on some remarks he would deliver to the bear, just before the knocking-around part began. In his fantasy he would burst into the clearing, where Bear would be busy with some small thing. "A word!" he would say, "A word, Bear, and right now, if you don't mind. Let me tell you about cougars!" he would say. "Cougars don't like jokes. Nor tricks played on them. They have little sense of humor, because life is a serious matter, Bear, and so is time." Cougar was fast working himself into a fever when from out of the sky an enormous crow dropped like a bullet in front of him. It swooped around the big cat's head and landed on a branch just at Cougar's eye level and blocking his way. No one had ever confronted Cougar before, not bird nor beast, and the sheer audacity of the crow stopped him in his tracks. He remained there, frozen in mid-stride with one foot up in the air.

"Where do you think you're going?" the crow asked quietly.

"What's it to you?" asked Cougar.

The crow pointed a warning wing at Cougar. "No foolishness," he said steadily, "Just answer the question."

"I'm going home," said Cougar casually, deciding for the moment not to antagonize the bird.

"That would be a mistake," said the crow.

"Who says so?" said Cougar.

"You are on a mission," said the crow. "You were told to do something, were you not?"

"*Asked*, would be more like it," said Cougar, with a touch of petulance. "I was *asked* to do something. Not *told*."

"And what was your response?"

"To what?" Cougar said, evasively.

"No games," said the crow.

"I said I would do it," Cougar admitted.

"Have you done so?"

"Not yet."

"When were you planning to?"

"At some later date."

"Not a good idea," said the crow, shaking his head.

"Who are you?" said Cougar. "Who are you, anyway?"

"If I were you, I would return to the rocks," said the crow, ignoring Cougar's question, "that's what I would do. I'd return to the rocks and think things over."

Cougar thought for a moment about giving the crow

a good sideswipe with his paw, which after all was still up in the air, but something in the crow's eye told him that it would probably not be a good idea.

"Listen, this is stupid," he said, throwing caution to the winds. "They sent me out searching for a citrus fruit. A walking citrus fruit in the middle of cold weather. Now that's nuts. Let's face it. Two whole days I've been out looking for an imaginary thing. But this is the end of it now. It's a lot of nonsense. I hate games, and I don't like being made the fool. Bear can find his own lemon if he wants one so badly."

"*Lemming*," said the crow.

"That's right," said Cougar.

"You were sent looking for a *lemming*."

"That's *right*," said Cougar, a little louder.

"*Lemming*," said the crow patiently. "Lemming the mammal. Not lemon the fruit."

"Ah," said Cougar.

"You see the difference," said the crow.

"Bear said lemon," Cougar said feebly.

"Not likely," said the crow. "Bear usually says exactly what he means. And while you were out searching for an imaginary fruit, or even abandoning that search, the real thing, the mammal, could be in serious jeopardy. And in your arrogance, or laziness, the search could conceivably have been lost, with serious consequences ensuing not only to the lemming, but to other parties as well. Do you think that might be true?"

"I heard lemon," said the Cougar defensively.

"You heard wrong," said the crow. "One is brown with fur, the other smooth and yellow. And now, if you want some free advice; what I would do, if I were you, and right now, would be to turn yourself around and walk briskly to the rocks you were languishing on, the rocks that you were *guided* to, *sent* to, and gently pick up the *lemming* you offered to find, and bring it carefully back to the clearing and the bear. Do you understand?"

"Yes," said Cougar sheepishly.

"Do you think you are capable of doing all that?"

"I think so," said Cougar.

"Then do it quickly, and I promise no mention will be made of your stupidity and arrogance. And please, no further mistakes. I am not as forgiving as the bear."

Cougar nodded and started to slink off. "Cat!" the crow called out, "You will be watched!" he warned gravely, and Cougar strode rapidly away with an odd sideways motion, anxious to get as far away from the bird as possible.

The crow watched Cougar imperiously until the cat walked out of sight. Once or twice Cougar looked back to see if the bird was still there, and each time he took a furtive glance, he saw the crow staring at him unmoving and fearless. It was a sight that he would not soon forget. It was bad enough to have admitted wanting the company of a bear. Bad enough to have demeaned himself by offering his services to another animal, but then for the bear to have sent spies out to check on him—to assume that the mission would be mishandled and aborted, that was too much. And what was even more humiliating, what was almost beyond thinking about, was having been ordered around by a—he could hardly get the words out—ordered around by a bird! Argghh! Cougar shuddered with self-revulsion. It was an event probably unique in the history of cats. He began to imagine legends being told about him centuries from now. He would achieve world fame finally, but for all the wrong reasons. At this moment, the crow was probably recounting the event somewhere, to one of his cronies, the two of them chortling together and mindlessly poking one another in the ribs. The crow would talk, there was no question about that. Word would get out. It would be all over the forest in no time. Well, there were no witnesses; he could always say that the crow was lying.

One thing was certain, though, and that was that the crow would pay. Sooner or later the crow would pay for the affront. And so would the bear. There was no question about that. When and how would be saved for a later date.

Feeling put upon and martyred, he made his way back to the rocks, hoping not to find anything, for no other reason than to prove the crow wrong. But when he got there, he immediately discovered what he had been sent to find. Half hidden in a clump of dried leaves there was indeed a lemming, or what was left of one. The creature was unconscious, and so emaciated that at first Cougar thought it was dead. But upon closer examination he found a faint pulse in the scrawny body. Cougar picked it up by the scruff of the neck and headed home, feeling very proud of himself for what he had accomplished through his own courage and perseverance.

CHAPTER 2

Cougar set out at a fast pace and kept at it relentlessly, and for a time the physical effort stopped him from thinking any more abut his peculiar mission. But his nature was to question. Cougar would gnaw at problems, and wrestle with them, and pull at them, and tear at them, and in the end tangle them into such a snarl that there would be nothing left to do but walk away from the mess in disgust and never approach that particular issue again. As a result, he fought the impulse to ask questions as long as he could. He knew enough about himself to realize that things never got solved, and yet, somewhere in the middle of an event, his curiosity would come alive. Fighting it would cause an ache in his stomach that after a while became unbearable, so he would eventually give in and ask questions. The familiar ache was starting to present itself now.

What in God's name did the bear want with this mangy rodent? he wondered. This half-dead, disease-ridden, moth-eaten remnant? The answer was probably something boring and obvious. And why did the bear have to make such a mystery out of everything? Gazing into the clouds, whispering, taking long pauses. Why couldn't he simply have said, "Hey, Cougar, do me a favor, will you? A friend of mine is sick on a rock two days from here. Do you want to go and get him for me? I'd really appreciate it." Then Cougar could have said no, and that would have been the end of it.

Instead, here he was in the middle of something convoluted and stupid. Wasting his time and energy. Well, he would think no more about it.

But he could not stop thinking. As the trip progressed, he tried to wake the lemming from his delirium in order to get some information. He started by singing to himself, quietly at first and then quite loudly, but all that happened was that the lemming would call out things in alarm from some other time, some other place, and when Cougar would try to pick up the thread, the lemming would doze off again in a feverish fog. Once or twice Cougar dropped the lemming, almost by accident, thinking this might get him to wake up long enough for a few simple questions. The first time he was dropped, the lemming called out, "Help! Help! I'm going under!"

"Under what?" Cougar asked with great interest, "What are you going under?" The lemming mumbled something incoherent, so Cougar picked him up and dropped him again.

"I can't swim!" the lemming shouted, "I can't swim!"

"What do you mean?" said Cougar, "Why can't you swim?" But the lemming was off somewhere, and no amount of nudging and rolling around could bring him back.

Cougar finally gave up in disgust and continued on in silence, hoping fervently that the lemming would wake up with a lot of questions that he could ignore.

On the afternoon of the second day, the lemming's fever broke, and he came out of a delirious sleep filled with nightmares of all descriptions to find that he was dangling from the jaws of an enormous beast. At first he thought that he was still dreaming, but the pain in his neck at the point he was being held soon let him know that he was awake. His head was tilted toward the ground at an awkward angle, but he could make out his captor's feet as he walked along, so he knew immediately that the animal was one of the big cats. This discovery did not make him happy about his chances for survival. The grip that he was held by was firm and yet careful, which meant that the cat knew he was alive. Surely then the cat also knew he was feverish. But why would the cat have wanted a sick animal for his prey? One that put up no resistance and offered no real nourishment? The lemming started to speculate about the cat's possible plans for him, but he quickly forced himself to stop. Worrying about the future would only make him tense, and at all costs he needed to remain calm now. It would be better for him if the cat did not know he was awake, so he concentrated on breathing very slowly, and steeled himself for the task of remaining completely still for what could possibly be a long period of time. Sooner or later, with any luck, the cat would change his grip, or put him down for a moment for a short rest or some water, and his work would be to remain alert so that whatever energy he had could be summoned for a possible leap to safety. "And then what?" he asked himself, and immediately fell into depression. "Where will you go then? What future is there for you? Who will you share it with?" The lemming thought back over his short life, and it seemed to him that it had consisted of nothing but continuous loneliness and fear. Running madly from one terrible situation to another, with only enough time between horrors to catch his breath, wonder what it was all about, and then dash madly on again. "Enough of that," he said sharply to himself. There'd be plenty of time to get depressed when he survived this mess. If he survived it. With all his will, the lemming went back to concentrating on his breathing, and precarious as his situation was, as he swung back and forth from the mouth of the cat, listening to the soft padding of his feet and being warmed by each exhalation of the cat's breath, he dozed off again.

The next time he woke up he was on the ground. Without moving a muscle, without daring to open his eyes, he strained his senses to try and get some feel for his surroundings. The sound of water filled his ears, and he guessed that the cat had put him down so that he could take a drink. He strained his hearing and made out lapping sounds from nearby. Then cautiously he opened one eye and there, just as he had hoped, was the cat, with his back toward him, drinking from a small stream. "This is it," the lemming decided, knowing that if he wanted to escape this could very well be his only chance. With half-closed eyes he surveyed the terrain for a direction to follow and slowly gathered his feet beneath him, readying himself for a dash. Close by there was a huge fallen tree, and with luck there would be a burrow underneath and perhaps a tunnel network that would enable him to lose the cat. He swallowed, took a deep breath, pushed off with all his strength, and at that instant a blood-curdling scream filled his ears. In mid-leap the lemming knew that it was all over. A heavy paw came down on him, claws out like a steel cage, and the lemming smashed down into the earth.

"Don't do it," said the cat, from a place of terrible pain and restraint. "Don't leave, don't even think about it. I can't tell you how upset I would be if I had to go out looking for you again." The cat's eyes were wild, his voice was shaking, and his heart was pounding like thunder. The lemming had heard stories of the big cats. He'd always had an idea of what to expect, so the restraint that he was witnessing was awesome and spellbinding. "I'm close to the edge," the cat went on. "Don't push me over. I don't want to hurt you. I just want to deliver you and go about my business. I made a promise to the bear, and I intend to keep it. But no one said dead or alive. Do you follow me? That wasn't mentioned in the deal. So if you even *think* about running out on me again, the bear will be presented with an empty lemming carcass, and I'll be singing a song. Do I make myself clear?"

The lemming nodded frantically.

"I didn't HEAR YOU!" the cat roared, completely losing all his earlier restraint. Every muscle in his body shook and his hair stood up on end.

"It's clear! It's clear!" said the lemming.

"I'm glad we understand each other," said the cat. He picked up the lemming in his teeth, took a deep breath, and continued on his way. In the minutes that followed, the cat tried valiantly to calm himself down, and the lemming slowly took in his bout with a hurricane. There had been no time for fear. The sights and sounds had been so awesome that the lemming found himself more in a state of admiration for the laws of nature than he did in any jeopardy. The cat's anguish seemed so profound that he forgot his own troubles momentarily, and began wondering what was eating the poor creature. Strangely, he even felt somehow responsible for the cat's torment, though for the life of him he couldn't understand how or why. It was clear that he wasn't simply dinner. Something else was at play here. Something about being delivered to a bear, the cat had said. What could that possibly mean?

"I'm sorry if I upset you," he said cautiously, his curiosity getting the better of him.

"Forget it," said the cat.

"I woke up from a stupor and there I was hanging from your teeth," said the lemming. "You can probably imagine what went through my mind."

"Right," said the cat, obviously not interested in pursuing the conversation.

"That's why I ran off," said the lemming. "I wasn't sure of your intentions."

"Right."

The lemming questioned the wisdom of continuing, but he couldn't stop himself. "Forgive me if I'm being too inquisitive," he said politely, "but earlier did you say something about a bear?"

"Right," said the cat.

"Something about taking me to a bear, I thought I heard."

"That's right," the cat answered.

"Hmmm—" said the lemming with much expression, hoping that the intensity of his musing would encourage the cat to open up a little, but it didn't have the desired effect.

"I wonder what a bear would want with me," he said theoretically. Still no response from the cat. It was dangerous to continue; he could feel the cat chafing at his questions, but the strangeness of the situation drove him on.

"It's an interesting thing to think about, isn't it?" he ventured. There was still no response, and a new anxiety crossed the lemming's mind.

"To the best of my knowledge, bears are vegetarians. Would you happen to know if that's true?"

"Sometimes a fish," the cat said curtly.

"I see—" said the lemming, "sometimes a fish. You can probably understand my concern. I've never met a bear, never even seen one; so to hear you remark that a bear has some business with me is slightly disconcerting. I'm sure that's a pretty normal reaction, wouldn't you say?" Each mention of the bear caused the cat to bristle and tense up, but the lemming couldn't stop himself from pressing further. "It's an interesting speculation, isn't it?" he asked, "what a bear would want with a lemming?"

No answer from the cat.

"You wouldn't know, by any chance, would you?"

"Let's get off this, all right?" said the cat. "I don't know what he wants with anything."

"I didn't mean to intrude," said the lemming. "I was just under the impression that you worked for him."

"I don't work for anybody," said the cat.

"You just run errands for him," said the lemming.

"Not bloody likely," said the cat, "A favor is more like it. I'm doing him a favor."

"That's kind of unusual, isn't it?" asked the lemming, hoping that he'd finally gotten a foothold. "I didn't know cats did favors for anybody."

"It's not your everyday occurrence," the cat replied grudgingly.

"Funny," said the lemming.

"What is?" asked the cat.

"Oh, it just seems a little odd. You're doing favors for a bear when you don't even seem to like him very much."

"He's an ingrate!" the cat exploded, momentarily losing his grip on the lemming. "He's arrogant and he's haughty and he can't be trusted. Does that sound likable to you? Do you like that type?"

"No, I don't," said the lemming.

"Neither do I," said the cat. "He's deceitful, and he's cunning, and he manipulates, and I don't want to talk about him any more."

"I don't blame you," said the lemming. They walked on for a while in silence, and then the lemming began chuckling to himself somewhat theatrically.

"What is it?" asked the cat. "What's so funny?"

"Oh, nothing," said the lemming. He was silent for a while and then began chuckling again. The cat stopped walking and looked down at the lemming.

"I said, 'What's so funny?' "

"Oh, it's nothing really. I was just imagining what would happen if you let me go. I got a picture of this bear waiting endlessly for us to show up, and then finding out years later that we'd gone our separate ways! It just struck me as being very amusing!"

"Nice try," said the cat, and he started walking again.

The air went out of the lemming. All the performing stopped, and he just hung limply from the cat's mouth. "I don't understand," he said bleakly. "You're a cat. Why do you do things for this bear? Why do you do favors for him if you hate him so much?"

The cat thought for a long time before answering. "He has powers," said the cat. "He knows things. I want to know what he knows."

The hair went up on the lemming's neck, and dark

fantasies began to fill his mind. Who was this bear? he thought to himself. A bear who can control the big cats? Who can make them run errands and fill them with fear? And if the bear has such a terrible hold on this great and powerful cat, what possible chance would he have?

CHAPTER 3

On the evening of the second day, they arrived at the clearing. It was empty and still except for a duck who was sweeping the area with great vigor. Cougar dropped his charge ceremoniously and waited for some sign of approval from the duck, some acknowledgment of his great accomplishment, but none was forthcoming. The duck was sweeping passionately, raising great clouds of dust and creating more mess than she was removing. Cougar coughed to catch her attention, but the duck's mind was on her work. "Say, you!" Cougar called out. "Marion! Have you seen the bear?"

The duck stopped sweeping momentarily. "Oh, hello, Romo," she said politely, "Yes, I have. He's resting in his quarters."

"Quarters, eh?" said Cougar, amused at her choice of words. He picked up the lemming and started moving off.

"I don't think he wants to be disturbed!" the duck called out in alarm, but Cougar paid no attention. He had spent four days running the bear's errands, and he'd disturb him if he felt like it. He walked out of the clearing and back into the woods. When he reached the mouth of the bear's cave he paused, wondering whether or not to dare enter, and decided that on this particular occasion he would not. Someday he would enter the cave. He knew that. Someday he would penetrate at least this one mystery, but something told him that today was not the day for it. So he dropped the lemming roughly on the ground and flopped down at the entranceway with an enormous yawn loud enough to announce his presence not only to the bear, but to every living thing within twenty miles. There was a rustling from inside the cave, and Cougar whipped to attention. Sounds could be heard from deep within, clumsy shuffling sounds, then soft murmurings, then an odd kind of sing-song crooning. The sounds got nearer and nearer, and then at the mouth of the cave appeared the largest animal that the lemming had ever seen. It was a bear to end all bears. A slow, deliberate creature of enormous size and bulk. The lemming looked on in amazement as he shuffled back and forth at the entranceway to his cave, doing a slow sort of dance. He did not really look at his visitors, yet it was clear that he was keenly aware of them. In the bear's movement there was a sense of great dormant power, but there was also something gentle about him, something graceful, almost dainty, which oddly enough, even added to the feeling of his enormous strength. Still mumbling to himself the bear slowly sat down. He coughed, and a small bird flew out of his mouth, ricocheted into the dirt, and then flapped away. Neither the bear nor the cat seemed to find it unusual. The bear slowly shifted his gaze over to the lemming.

"What is it you want?" asked the bear softly.

The lemming looked vacantly at the bear, and then over at the cat for some sign of what to do, but the cat looked back just as blankly, blinked twice and then looked away, his eyes glazing over just slightly.

"What do I want?" asked the lemming.

"Yes, what do you want?"

"I don't want anything," said the lemming.

"Then you have come to the wrong place," said the bear. He got up and slowly started back into his cave.

"Wait a minute," said Cougar, with the beginnings of a whimper in his voice. "Wait a minute, Bear, please. Here's your lemming. This is him. The lemming you sent me for."

"Yes, I know all about it," said the bear with a hard look at the cat. "Do you think I have a memory problem?"

"No," said Cougar, squirming uncomfortably. "But you just asked him what he wants."

"So I did," said the bear. "Was that an impertinent question? Was my tone perhaps disrespectful?"

"No, not at all," said Cougar, "But why should you ask him what he wants? You sent for him. You asked me to bring him to you. You see my meaning."

"I said, 'Find the lemming. He'll be headed in our direction.' I believe those were my words."

"So they were," said Cougar. "So they were. Your *exact* words, in fact. And I *did* find him, and here he is."

"What does he want?" the bear asked Cougar. Cougar tried to answer. His mouth moved up and down for a while but nothing came out.

Bear sighed his weary sigh, looked heavenward, and went back into his cave. The lemming, having nothing else to do, stared into the darkness for a while, and then stole a glance at the cat whose face was starting to scrunch up like he'd been eating a lemon. His eyes were bulging and his muscles began to twitch, and his whole body stiffened, and for a moment the lemming feared that he would explode. Then the cat let out an enormous scream, and with all four legs rigid he leaped straight into the air. Then he fell down and started rolling around in the dirt, kicking out wildly in every direction and screaming at the top of his lungs. Then just as quickly he stopped, got up, took a long look into the cave and ran off into the woods with a lopsided drunken gait. His screaming began again soon afterward and could be heard long into the night.

The lemming kept staring at the mouth of the cave. It was all very odd, he thought. Cats who ran errands, bears who spat birds—strange behavior on all sides. But he was alive and safe for the moment, that much he could say. He took at deep breath and realized that this was the first moment in his memory that he didn't feel in immediate jeopardy. Why was that? he wondered. Things were no more familiar or comfortable here than any place he'd fallen into since leaving home. When was that? Weeks ago? Months ago? He couldn't even remember. But he was somehow at ease at this moment, and the feeling was so unusual that he didn't quite trust it. Why don't I trust it? he asked himself. Was it something in the place, or something in myself? An interesting question, he decided; but one that required more time and energy than he was interested in expending at the moment. He lay down and looked up at the sky. The first stars were beginning to twinkle. He thought about what to do and where to go, and nothing particular came to mind. "What do you want?" the bear had asked. He didn't have a clue. Well, that wasn't exactly true. Something to eat would be a good start. He began to recognize how terribly hungry and thirsty he was, and couldn't remember how many days it had been since he'd had any food at all. Perhaps that was all the bear had meant by his question. Maybe if he'd had the courage to say he was hungry the bear would have simply given him a morsel of food and that would have been the end of it. As he thought about it, he suspected that the bear probably would have given him something to eat, and yet he didn't think that's what he really had in mind.

At that moment a very distinct smell drifted toward him. A warm porridge kind of smell, and it made the lemming feel alive in places he had forgotten existed. It was coming from the direction of the clearing, and the lemming thought it might be a good idea to wander back in that general direction, just to see what was going on. At the clearing the duck was vigorously stirring a huge cauldron of soup, which was sitting on an open fire. Much of what she stirred was slopping over the sides, but she seemed not to mind.

"Oh," she said as she saw him, "You startled me. Hello! Welcome!"

"Thank you," said the lemming.

He sat down beneath a huge pine tree at the far end of the clearing hoping fervently that the duck would notice his look of worship directed at the soup, but her nose was to the grindstone. The lemming tried some quiet coughing, which made the duck look up at him, and his mournful expression and emaciated appearance immediately touched her heart.

"What's wrong with you?" she asked, "You sound terrible."

"I'm not well," said the lemming.

"I should think not," said the duck. "Look at you. When's the last time you ate?"

"I don't remember."

"You don't *remember?*"

"No."

"My God," she said, shaking her head, "He doesn't remember when he ate." She waddled over to the cauldron, dipped a wooden bowl into the soup, and brought it over to the lemming. Before she handed it to him, she grabbed him swiftly by the nose. "Dry as a bone," she said. "You should take better care of yourself."

"I'm doing the best I know how," said the lemming, taking the soup from her and digging into it greedily.

The duck waddled back to her cauldron. "That's what everyone says. Everyone thinks they're doing the best they know how, and yet look at them." The lemming ate furiously. He was too hungry to taste anything, but he knew it was the best food he'd ever had. He could feel the warmth and goodness of it flowing like lava into nooks and crannies of his body that he thought had been dead.

As he was finishing the bowl and getting ready to ask for more, he heard a strange sound from the direction of the cave. It was a low "mooing" kind of sound, starting almost inaudibly, but it soon built up into something intense and weird. Something like wind blowing through a canyon in the dead of night. That or someone groaning in the middle of an important nightmare.

"What's this, now?" he thought. He looked over the duck, but it didn't seem to trouble her, so he kept on eating. The sound immediately got louder, and before long it turned into a rumbling kind of howl. The lemming tried with all his might to mind his own business and concentrate on the food, but the awesome sound was beginning to make waves in his soup, and he could feel the ground rumbling beneath him. "Someone is killing the bear," the lemming said to himself, "He's being tortured to death." Still there was no sign from the duck. He tried for a while longer to pretend he didn't hear it but it became too much for him.

"What is that? What's that noise?" he finally asked.

"It's the bear," replied the duck.

"What is it? What's he doing?" the lemming asked.

"He's doing his 'hum,' " the duck answered pleasantly.

"What's a hum?" the lemming asked.

"What is it?" said the duck. "Well, it's hard to explain. A hum is a hum."

"What does he do it for?" asked the lemming, trying to keep his soup from flying out of the bowl, "Is it singing? What is it?"

"No, it's not singing," said the duck. "He does it to— it's very hard to put into words. He does it to shake his brains loose."

"To do what?" the lemming asked, hoping he hadn't heard correctly.

"To shake his brains loose," the duck repeated.

"Why does he want to shake his brains loose?" asked the lemming.

"So he can get away from his bear."

"So he can get away from what bear?" asked the lemming.

"From his own bear."

"From what own bear?"

"From the bear that he is."

"How can he get away from the bear that he is?"

The duck looked at him in pity and disbelief. "Well, that's the point of everything, isn't it? I have to get away from my duckness, he has to get away from his bearness, you have to get away from your—" All of a sudden she really saw him. "What are you?" she asked.

"I used to be a lemming."

"What are you now?"

"I don't know what I am now."

"Well that's either quite wonderful or the saddest thing I've ever heard," said the duck, folding her wings over her heart and tipping her head to one side.

"It's not sad or wonderful," said the lemming, "It's just the way things are."

"What way are things?" asked the duck.

"What things?"

"The things that are the way they are. What way are they?" asked the duck.

"They are different ways," the lemming answered.

"My point exactly," said the duck.

The lemming shook his head briskly, trying to clear it out. "Wait a minute,"he said, "what are we talking about? I've kind of lost the track here."

"We're talking about *being*," said the duck. "We're talking about *essences*. And I was saying that you have to get away from your lemmingness."

"I *am* away from my lemmingness," said the lemming.

"I don't think so," said the duck with conviction.

"I am. I'm well away from it."

"I'm sorry to say that you're not," said the duck.

"How do you know?" the lemming asked, a touch of annoyance creeping into his voice. "Two minutes ago you didn't even know what a lemming was. How can you say that I'm away from my lemmingness if you don't even know what lemmings are?"

"I don't have to know what lemmings are," said the duck. "I can see you."

"So what?" said the lemming. "I can see you too."

"And what do you see?" the duck asked, posing grandly, with her neck craned and her wings spread wide.

"I see a duck. A plain duck."

"Then you are blind."

"You think so?" asked the lemming."

It is my sad duty to inform you that you are blind," said the duck formally.

"If you're not a duck, what are you?"

"I am a lion," said the duck. "If you had eyes, that's what you would see."

"You are a lion?" the lemming asked cautiously.

"That is correct."

"A big golden thing, with a mane?" asked the lemming.

"That's right."

"A lion, like the one who brought me here."

"Goodness no," said the duck vehemently, "Romo is a cat! He's about as far from being a lion as I don't know what."

The discussion was beginning to give the lemming a headache, and he longed for silence, but he decided to behave himself at least till he had another bowl of soup. Then he would thank her kindly and go about his business.

"You look confused," the duck said with compassion. "So was I when I first came here. It won't last long. The bear will clear away the cobwebs, wait and see. As the months go by you'll become less agitated and more at peace."

"I'm not agitated for the reasons you think," said the lemming.

"Why are you agitated?" asked the duck.

"Whatever reasons you think, those are not the reasons that I'm agitated," said the lemming sharply.

"Oh yes they are!" said the duck breezily. "Otherwise you wouldn't be so upset. Look at you!"

"What right do you have to tell me who I am?" said the lemming, unable to contain his annoyance. "You don't know me, you've never seen me before, and here you're giving me a rundown on my entire existence. And I'm not staying here either, if that's what you think. I was brought here by mistake but I'll be leaving on purpose as soon as I finish my soup."

"Oh, I doubt that," said the duck laughing easily.

"You do, eh?"

"Well, you've come all this way."

"Not by *choice*," said the lemming. He was starting to shout a little now. "I was *captured*. I was brought here against my will in a delirium fever!"

"But you are *here*, nevertheless, aren't you?"

"So what?"

"Well, that, my dear, simply speaks for itself, doesn't it?" said the duck with an air of finality. She folded her wings behind her, craned her neck forward and smiled sweetly as if waiting for the lemming to concede defeat.

"And what exactly does it say?" the lemming sputtered, giving up nothing.

"It says, quite simply, that this is where you are supposed to be."

"And how did you come to that conclusion? Why should I want to be here?"

"You came here to see the bear, obviously, why don't you admit it?"

"You have it backward. I didn't want to see the bear, he wanted to see me. And then once he saw me, he changed his mind." The lemming got up in a huff and, throwing caution to winds, poured himself another bowl of soup.

"Bear doesn't do that," said the duck seriously. "He doesn't change his mind."

"This time he changed his mind."

"How do you know?"

"Because when I was introduced to him, he asked me what I wanted. That's how I know. Why would he ask me what I wanted if *he* wanted to see *me*?"

"What did you answer?"

"What was there to answer? I didn't want anything, and that's what I told him."

"You told him you didn't want anything? You actually said that?"

"Yes I did. That's what I said."

"A serious mistake," said the duck.

"Listen," said the lemming, throwing in the sponge, "let me be honest with you. I don't have the vaguest idea in the world what you are talking about. I didn't ask for all this philosophy. You gave me two bowls of soup and for that I thank you, but if I knew they came with a lecture I think I might have stayed hungry."

The duck looked at him squarely and clinically. "It's clear now why you are a lemming," she said.

"I'm not a lemming. I told you that already."

"Yes, you told me that, but it's not true. You've stopped living with lemmings, but you are a lemming nevertheless."

"What right do you have to tell me what I am?" said the lemming, his voice rising in great indignation. "You don't know what's inside me!"

"True enough," said the duck, "but the bear knows what's inside you, and that's why he asked you what you wanted."

"Oh, *yes*?" shouted the lemming.

"Yes."

"Well, if he could see inside me he wouldn't have to ask me what I wanted. He would *know*. Wouldn't he!" The lemming sat back and folded his arms, sure that the argument was now over.

"He was being polite," said the duck easily. "He didn't want to frighten you."

The lemming searched his mind for something to hurl back at her, but he was too tired to fight anymore.

Nothing seemed to penetrate her smugness. What is wrong with her? he wondered, and why does she get my goat so much? Are all ducks this dense, or is she a special case? He felt like strangling her, and that wasn't like him at all. He was a peaceful soul. At least he had been till he met this duck.

A shadow crossed his line of vision. He looked up and saw the bear sitting to one side of the cauldron, absorbed in his own thoughts and paying no apparent attention to his surroundings or the heated discussion. But how long had he been there? And how did he arrive so silently, with no one seeing him?

The lemming decided not say anything further. He was after all a guest at this place, whatever it was, and it might be wise not to antagonize his host, if he hadn't done so already.

CHAPTER 4

After what seemed like an eternity, the bear slowly raised his head, looked over at the lemming and smiled slightly. The smile was warm and friendly, and the lemming slowly exhaled. Whatever problem he anticipated did not materialize.

"Still here?" asked the bear.

"Yes, I seem to be," the lemming answered.

"That's good. That's good," the bear said warmly, nodding to no one in particular. "Has Marion cleared up everything for you? Who you are? Where you're going?"

"Not really," said the lemming cautiously.

"Give her a bit more time," said the bear.

"We just had a little chat," said the duck, blushing right through to her feathers.

"Yes, I'm sure you did," said the bear in a tone that the lemming couldn't quite make out. It was still friendly, but had an undercurrent of something else. The duck was digging a small hole in the ground with one foot.

"I see you've found your tree," said the bear.

"Excuse me?" said the lemming.

"Your tree. You've found your tree," the bear said amiably, waving a paw at the tree that the lemming was sitting beneath.

"What tree is that?" asked the lemming.

"The one you're leaning on," said the bear.

The lemming looked round at the huge pine that he had settled under. "Oh yes," he said. "The tree. Well, I found a tree. I don't know if it's mine or not."

"Oh, it's yours all right," said the bear, "It's been waiting for you for quite some time, too."

"Oh, yes," said the lemming, "My tree. Thank you for letting me rest under it."

"Don't thank me," said the bear, "it's your tree. If you're going to thank anyone, thank the tree."

It was of course a joke, so the lemming laughed. But the expression on the bear's face indicated that he didn't share the humor.

The lemming decided that it might not be a bad idea to comply with the bear's suggestion, so he turned around to the great pine and under his breath muttered, "Thank you, tree."

"Good, good," said the bear joyfully. "It was a little miffed at having been ignored, but it's all right now."

The lemming nodded longer than necessary. What was there to say?

"It's good to thank the trees we lean on," said the bear. "It's a habit worth cultivating."

"I'll try to remember that."

They sat in silence, each eating their soup, with the duck to one side waiting for unspoken commands from the bear. Periodically the bear's mind would drift off somewhere, and the duck would raise his bowl to keep the soup from spilling all over him. At these moments he would return briefly from wherever he had gone, and look over at the lemming with a kind of stupefied smile on his face. The lemming would smile back, without much behind it, and as he became a little more comfortable he began to examine this bear, trying to fit the animal in front of him with the cat's description. "He has powers," the cat had said. "He knows things." Well, perhaps some other bear knew things, not this one. This poor creature didn't even have the power to feed himself without falling asleep and slopping over everything. The strangest thing of all was that the cat had even seemed afraid of him. In his presence the cat had actually seemed shaken and cowed. That was completely incomprehensible. Even the lemming, who was afraid of almost everything wasn't afraid of this sad case, lost somewhere in a fog, or a dream, oblivious to most of his surroundings.

"Have you found out what you want?" the bear asked suddenly, shaking the lemming out of his reverie.

"No, not yet, I'm afraid."

"I see you have some soup," said the bear, waving languidly in its general direction.

"Yes," said the lemming, "the duck was kind enough to give me a bowl."

"Perhaps that was what you wanted," said the bear.

"Yes," said the lemming with forced enthusiasm, "maybe that's what I wanted!"

"It's a piddling little thing to want," said the bear.

"I suppose it is," said the lemming, "I suppose it is."

"There's a whole universe of things to want out there, and you wanted some soup. It's a little sad."

"Well, I was practically starving," said the lemming, "I'm not sure if that's what I want in the ultimate scheme of things, but when you're hungry you think of food."

"Some do, some don't," said the bear.

"Well, I think probably more do than don't," said the lemming.

"Perhaps, perhaps not," said the bear.

"I think that as a general rule, in times of hunger, most of us would go for some food," the lemming said. It was a ridiculous discussion, and he wasn't about to feel guilty about wanting something to eat when he was starving.

"General rules don't interest me much," said the bear.

"Why is that?" asked the lemming, praying that this wasn't going to be another discussion like the one he'd just had with the duck.

"I think we use them as a cover. They're good things to hide behind."

"I don't follow you."

"Well, take your basic lemming, for instance. As a general rule they tend to take flying leaps into the ocean and kill themselves."

"I beg your pardon?" said the lemming, not sure he'd heard right.

"Lemmings," said the bear. "They throw themselves off high places."

"There are those lemmings that don't do that," said the lemming indignantly. The bear was getting a bit personal now, for a perfect stranger. It was in questionable taste.

"My point exactly," said the bear, "There are a few lemmings here and there who don't leap off cliffs, but I think it's safe to say that as a general rule they mostly jump into the ocean."

"I don't know what you're getting at."

"I'm just trying to say that we have to be careful about general rules. It's not a bad idea to examine them. It's probably saved the life of a lemming or two here and there. It might even save yours someday."

"I suppose that's true," said the lemming. His own life was a testimony to that fact, there was no denying it, but he didn't want to be talking about it now, in this place, with strangers.

"For example," said the bear, "You're a lemming. Imagine a situation where you are surrounded by millions of lemmings and all of them are planning to kill themselves by jumping off cliffs and into the western sea. If it were me, I just might ask, 'Why? Why are we all doing this thing? Why do we want to kill ourselves by jumping off enormous cliffs?' But this line of questioning can make a lot of folks nervous, particularly if they're just gearing themselves up to jump. Their juices are telling them to go, and they're going. They want to do it. They don't have any real answers, they don't *want* any real answers. They just want to do what they want to do. So if you question too hard you end up forcing a lot of friends and relatives to say things that they don't quite believe in and that gets very embarrassing. That's why mostly everyone goes around quoting general rules. It keeps them from having to say what's really on their minds. A lot of lemmings would rather keep their mouths shut than offend anyone. But my own thinking is that in the long run it's probably better to ask unpopular questions and stay alive." The bear was musing as he spoke, looking at the moon, and it was all very casual, but what he was talking about was getting very close to events in the lemming's own life. Things that had actually happened to him. Did the bear know that, or was he just rambling around, hitting on things by accident? It was hard to tell.

"That's my opinion, anyway," the bear said. "What do you think? Does all this sound possible?"

"Yes," the lemming said cautiously.

"But you see, that presents other problems," said the bear.

"Like what?" the lemming asked.

"Well, for example, if I'd thought of myself as a lemming all my life, and my people started behaving in a strange and bizarre manner, I might start thinking that I was a misfit. I might get depressed and confused. I might try to be like them and botch it up and think that there was something wrong with me."

The lemming's heart began to beat like thunder. The bear was telling him his own life story. He was telling it as if it was theory, but it was the lemming's story. No one else's. It could not have been an accident. The bear was pretending that he was inventing it as he went along, but it wasn't possible. He knew who the lemming was, there was no doubt of it. The bear went on, "And on the other hand, what if this misfit wasn't strong enough to withstand the pressure? What if his instincts started to return just at the moment when the blood had risen in all of his people? And what if these instincts took him to the edge of death? And then what if some miracle kept him from following his people to their destiny into the sea? What would he think of himself then?"

"I don't know," said the lemming, and it was true. It was his own story that the bear was telling, but he was digging into it further than the lemming had.

"I think what would happen is this," said the bear. "I think I would recoil in horror at the whole idea of being a lemming. I would reject all lemmings. Anything connected with lemmings. I would deny that I'd ever been a lemming. Ever knew one."

The lemming was past wonder at this point. He sat nodding at each point the bear made, his mouth open wide and his body slouched over, glued to every word the bear uttered. His life was being read as profoundly as if the bear had ripped him open and plunged his paws into his stomach.

"I'd turn away from the sea and the madness, and I'd point myself in some direction that couldn't contain lemmings. That never saw a lemming. Never heard of them. I'd start a brand-new existence as something completely different, or try to. That's what I would do, I'd try to erase the memory of my family, my friends; I'd try to blot out my mother, my father, my sister, who were foolish enough to have been born lemmings, with lemming instincts, and who lived and died as lemmings; I'd try to erase the memory of all the faces and voices I grew up with, and all the lemming patterns of behavior I'd grown up with, some of which were terrible, and some that weren't so terrible; and I'd try to carve out a new existence. That's what I would do. What about you? What would you do?"

"That's what I would do," said the lemming, softly.

"And it would be the right idea, too, in a way," said the bear, "but it would be very hard. Very hard indeed. Because what would I be? I would be unlemming. That's what I would be. A non-thing. I'd have to eat un-lemming food. I'd have to sleep in un-lemming places. I'd have to go in un-lemming directions and think un-lemming thoughts. Wouldn't I?"

"Yes," said the lemming.

"And every time I began to do a lemming thing I would feel terror. 'Look out!' my mind would scream, 'A lemming thought! The next thing you know you'll be leaping off the nearest precipice! *No lemming thoughts,* my mind would scream at me, *not now, not ever!*' "

"And then I would call back, 'Can't I even think of my mother? My father? My sister?' "

" 'No,' my mind would say, 'They're jumpers. They run with the pack. They'll kill you too if you think about them at all. So—' " The bear said, and he shrugged sadly. "Where then would I go? What would I do?"

"I'd run," the lemming said.

"Yes, that's what I'd do too," said the bear, "I'd run as far from my past as my legs could carry me. And I'd keep on running until—" He paused.

"Yes?" asked the lemming.

"Well, that's the question, isn't it?"

The lemming nodded.

"What do you think the answer is?"

"I don't know."

"I'd run until my past caught me. That's what I would do. Do you understand that?"

"No."

"I'd run until my fear carried me in a circle right back to what I'd run from. In my panic I'd fall off a cliff, or into a pit, or a river or a lake, whether I knew how to swim or not, or failing that I'd fall into the mouth of some beast or other. One way or another I would confirm for myself my worst terrors. That I was indeed a lemming. A lemming in life, and a lemming in death." The bear shook his head sadly. "A terrible fate," he said. "Sad and terrible." He turned, finally, and faced his guest. "But there is another solution."

He said, "Do you know what it is?" The lemming shook his head.

"Run *toward* something!" The bear said, with a huge smile and his arms spread wide, and for a moment the lemming had the terrible thought that it was the end of what the bear had to say. That after the extraordinary build up, after taking him to an emotional precipice, the bear had nowhere to go, and he was to be left dangling in the discussion just as he was in life.

"Run toward something?" he asked plaintively.

"Run toward something!" The bear repeated emphatically.

"Do you have anything particular in mind?" the lemming asked.

"What do you want?" the bear asked, and his smile was gone.

"I want not to be a lemming."

"Not good enough. Look where that desire has brought you."

"I don't know what else to say. I feel empty and lost, and I don't want to be a lemming."

"You feel empty and lost, and you hope to fill up that emptiness by not being something. A good trick if you can do it. But if you manage it I think you'll be the first.

"I don't know what else to say."

"Well, perhaps you will someday," said the bear, and he started to leave.

"No, no, please don't go!" the lemming cried. "Help me! I need to know what to do. Everything you've said has been true. Somehow you can see inside me. I've been running, and I've been terrified for so long that I can't remember anything else. I don't want to go on this way, but I don't know what else to do." The lemming said, tears welling up in his eyes, "Please help me!"

"What are you?" the bear asked gently.

The lemming shook his head mournfully. "I don't know what I am," he said.

"Are you a lemming?"

"Yes, partly, but also I'm something else."

"What is it?"

"I don't know what it is."

"When are you a lemming?"

"When I do lemming things. Mindless and stupid things. Following instincts that I know will kill me."

"When are you not a lemming?"

The lemming looked deeply into himself, into places he had never examined before. "When I think. When I trust. When I feel there's a future."

"Then there is something in you worth knowing."

"I guess there is."

"What is it?"

"I don't know what it is."

"That's all right," said the bear, "you don't have to know that now. But there are other things you do know. Aren't there?"

"Yes," said the lemming.

"Do you know what you want?"

"I think so."

"What is it?"

"I want to know who I am," said the lemming.

"Finally," said the bear.

"I want to know the part of me that's not a lemming. The part of me that I can trust."

"Now you've said something," said the bear.

"Can you help me with that?" asked the lemming. "Is that why I'm here?"

"That's why we're all here," said the bear, and the lemming collapsed into the ground, sobbing his heart out, all the tension and terrors of a lifetime washing away into the soft piney earth of the clearing. The bear lumbered over to the lemming, tapped him gently on the back a few times, and then humming to himself, went back into his cave.

The duck watched the lemming weeping and was immediately filled with great compassion. She wanted to rush over and comfort him, but after the bad start they had made, she felt it would probably be better to leave him alone. It wasn't pain that he was feeling anyway. It was the release of pain. He'd be better in the morning. Oh, why couldn't she keep quiet! she asked, scolding herself harshly. Why did she have to butt into everything and everyone? Well, her intentions were good, she had to admit. She just couldn't stand to see anyone confused and suffering. It was all so unnecessary. Oh, she just wanted to shake critters sometimes! Shake them until they woke up into some sense. Either that or place them under a tree in a thunderstorm and have a big bolt of truth come down and light them up like a comet. "Oh, yes!" they'd say, all electric, with everything standing on end, "now I understand!" That's what she would like to do. But the bear would disapprove. He'd say that the electric treatment was good truth. Very good truth. But it would also kill you. "Patience, Marion," that's what the bear would say. "Patience. Slow and steady."

The lemming had stopped sobbing, so she waddled over to him, covered him with a wing as casually as she could and asked him if he wanted another bowl of soup, but he was already in another world.

CHAPTER 5

The next morning the lemming was awakened by the sounds of terrible shouting, and discovered that he was the one who was doing it. It had been a maelstrom of a night. A sea of turbulent dreams, dominated by an enormous bearlike creature, alternately spitting birds and thunderbolts. The bear kept running after the lemming protesting the warmest of intentions, wanting to give him great hugs, the way bears do, but the lemming knew that the life would be crushed out of him if he stopped running. At the end of the dream the bear had just caught him and something interesting was about to take place, but the lemming began screaming and woke himself up before it happened. Strange dream, he thought. And then as things stopped spinning, he remembered the evening before, and the actual bear. The one who really did spit birds and who gave him a very specific rundown of his own entire true life story. The lemming thought about this, and decided that the actual bear in the clearing was probably more disturbing than the dream. The cat was right. The bear in the clearing did have powers. He had powers to see into the lives of others. A disturbing idea, if used for the wrong purposes. With powers like that the bear would be capable of doing enormous damage if he wanted to. But the bear had seemed harmless enough, in spite of his enormous size and power and personal magnetism, or whatever it was. Perhaps the bear didn't know anything at all. Perhaps he had spies working for him, checking up on whoever came into the clearing, snooping into their past. No, that was ridiculous. What would be the point of that? And how could it be accomplished? It would take an army of spies working full time. Well, maybe he did have an army of spies working for him full time. How was he to know? It was unlikely, but certainly within the realm of possibility. Whatever the method, he knew the lemming's past. There was no getting away from it. And he was also able to draw out the lemming's deepest most personal desires. Desires so buried that the lemming didn't even know he had them until the bear questioned him. Strange, he thought. Eerie.

It was also true that the bear seemed eager to help him. Help him discover who he was. *Who he really was.* An interesting idea. The bear had made him feel that he was a real thing. That underneath the un-lemming was good and solid stuff. Sitting with the bear he had felt the possibility of this truth pressing on him very urgently, but now in the bright cold light of dawn he wasn't quite so sure. Nor did it even seem that important. He lay on the ground and slowly accustomed himself to his surroundings. There was no evidence of the duck, for which he was very grateful, since his brain was cotton wool. No sound either from the direction of the cave, another blessing. He didn't have the energy to face anything quite that intense right now. He tried to relax, but the questions of the night before kept pressing at him. "Who are you?" the bear had asked. And he asked it pointedly too. An answer was almost on the tip of his tongue, but something kept him from saying it. Something kept him from even thinking it. So he fell back into the comfort of "I don't know" and "I am an un-lemming." But the bear had something specific in mind. "We'll let it go for now," he had said. Now *that* one had a lot of implications, didn't it? "We'll let it go for now." He would let it go for now. Perhaps there was a reason for his being here, perhaps there wasn't. He'd stay a bit longer in any case. If nothing else the food was good, and he could regain a bit of his strength.

The lemming got up slowly, stretched, and noticed to his surprise that he felt wonderful. There was no trace of the illness that had threatened his life the night before. Not an ache, not a sniffle. No hint of the gnawing hunger that had been his companion for weeks. Having nothing else to do, he began aimlessly exploring the area and saw that in the daylight the clearing was quite beautiful. The density of the forest opened up slightly here; it was on the highest point of a long slow rise, and the sun filtered softly through the trees, warming the earth and giving everything a magical shimmer. Around the edge of the clearing, huge stone slabs tumbled this way and that, creating a kind of natural amphitheater. It was unusually quite, and the peace and stillness of this place on this beautiful morning felt very healing. At the edge of the clearing he pushed his way through some young saplings and saw a sight so beautiful that it made him gasp. In the far distance, past an endless sloping vista of plain, forest, and valley was a heavy ribbon of snow covered mountains that stretched as far as the eye could see. The entire length of the horizon was taken up by the reds and purples and diamond-blue white of this majestic sight. The mountains looked very far away, and the lemming had the distinct impression that he was looking down at them. That they were lower than where he was standing. But since they were snow covered, it meant that they were probably thousands of feet higher. How strange it was to be looking down at something that was actually higher than where he was. Life was full of paradoxes. And some of them, he was forced to admit, were wonderful.

CHAPTER 6

Hungry again, he walked back to the clearing, hoping that there might be something around to nibble on, if it didn't mean getting too involved with the duck. If she was there when he got back, he thought he'd probably rather skip breakfast than engage in another one of her meandering seminars. He felt too good now to humble himself, even if it meant going hungry for a while. Happily, the duck wasn't there when he returned, and he was just about to sit down and rummage through the caches of food stored near the cauldron, when an enormous stick rolled in from the woods. It stopped at the woodpile and then rolled back into the woods at a rapid clip. "What next?" said the lemming, blinking in disbelief. He went back to his rummaging, and a moment later the stick rolled back into the clearing, emitted an enormous sigh, and went limp. To his dismay the lemming saw that it wasn't a stick at all but a rather imposing snake. It had stretched itself straight out with its belly up, and was in such a gnarled and twisted condition that it might for all the world have been a tree branch. It was covered with cuts and bruises, lumps, bumps, and dents, and a bend or two that looked permanent. It was also shedding in several places and the new skin underneath looked raw and tender. It was altogether the sorriest sight the lemming had ever seen. But with all its peculiarities, it was still an eight-foot boa constrictor. The lemming's hair stood on end, and he stiffened in all his parts. He had been miraculously fortunate in never having encountered a snake before, but their abilities were well known to him. He decided to leave the area as quickly as possible, and began backing off. Ordinarily this would not have been a good idea. He'd be unable to see what he'd be stepping on, and a leaf or twig could give him away but he was not about to take his eyes off the reptile. He took a few cautious steps, trying to think himself invisible, and though he made no noise at all, the snake sensed someone in the vicinity and rotated its head to where the lemming was skulking.

"Howdy," it said easily.

"Morning," said the lemming.

The snake examined him carefully. "What's wrong with you?" he asked.

"Nothing," said the lemming.

"You're all hunched over."

"Sorry," said the lemming, and he made an attempt to look casual.

"Why are you standing like that?" asked the snake.

"That's the way I stand."

"You can get cramped up like that. It stops your blood supply. You'll get sick."

"No, I'm fine," said the lemming, "I feel loose and good." He tried to demonstrate how loose and good he felt, but it was a terrible parody. It would have fooled no one. The lemming tried to find some way of unlocking his muscles, but it was useless, so he stood there, smiling away and made of stone. The snake didn't seem dangerous, but who could tell? He looked like a physical wreck, but that could have been a cunning maneuver. There was no way of knowing.

"You get sick a lot, don't you?" asked the snake.

"I've had my share of illness."

"Your sickness is your tension. That's what causes it," said the snake.

"Well, it's probably a contributory factor."

"No, it's the whole reason. Go back and examine the roots of your sickness. You'll find that it's tension."

"I'll do that," said the lemming stiffly.

"Why are you tense?" the snake asked clinically.

"At this particular moment?"

"Yes. Now. Right now. Why are you tense?"

"Well, I haven't spoken to a lot of snakes, to tell you the truth," the lemming said tentatively. "Maybe that's it."

"How does it make you feel?" asked the snake.

"Oh, you know," said the lemming evasively.

"I know," said the snake, "I want to see if *you* know. How does it make you feel?"

"Well—tense, I'd say. Yes, tense. Tense would be the word."

"Why is that?"

"Oh, you know," said the lemming with a nervous giggle. "Instant death, things like that."

"Ah-hah." said the snake, nodding sagely, "so when you look at me a red flag goes up in your mind. Something inside you yells out, 'Snake! Snake!' "

"That's the general idea, yes."

"Well, that's your problem."

"I don't see it as a problem."

"You don't, eh?" said the snake in a somewhat belligerent tone. "You're sick all the time!"

"I didn't say that," said the lemming. "I said I've been sick. That's not the same as being sick all the time."

"In any case, that's the reason for your sickness."

"What is?" asked the lemming, losing track of things again. "Tension in the presence of danger? That's the reason for my sickness?"

"That's the reason for all sickness. I'm just using you as an example."

"I see it more as staying alive."

"Well, that's nonsense," said the snake.

"It's not nonsense," the lemming shouted, "look at

you. You're a snake! When I see you my mind yells out 'Snake! Snake!' What's it supposed to yell out? 'Beaver? Beaver?'" He was getting upset in spite of himself. He knew it was dangerous, but he couldn't stand any more analysis from lunatics.

"Well, you've hurt my feelings now," said the snake, "and I don't understand your belligerent attitude, either."

The lemming thought for a moment that he would lose his mind. "I tell you the truth," he said, as patiently as he was able, "I don't understand the rules around here. I'm a rodent. You're a snake. That should be a sufficient enough explanation for my anxiety."

"What I'm trying to tell you," said, "is that you're not using your eyes."

"Are you going to tell me you're a lion? Is that what I'm about to hear?"

"Look at me for a minute," said the snake, "use your eyes. I haven't got a tooth in my head. I can't see out of one eye. I ache in all my joints. I have chronic pleurisy and half a stomach. On top of which, here I am at the clearing. I'm working my tail off to face the world with my head up, to straighten myself out. After years of diligent work, things start to look possible for me. I begin to think that maybe, just maybe the bear know what he's talking about. Once in a while I have a moment of relative peace and happiness. I can count birds and mice as my close personal friends. And then you come along and yell 'Snake! Snake!' How is that supposed to make me feel? Good? Maybe I'm not so happy with being a snake myself. Maybe I don't want to be a snake even more than you don't want me to be a snake. Did you ever stop to think about that?"

"No," said the lemming, with his head hung low.

"Use your eyes," said the snake. "Just use your eyes. And then link them up with your brain."

"I'll try to do that," said the lemming sadly.

"All kinds of things go on here," said the snake. "Try to stay loose."

"I'll keep it in mind," said the lemming.

"It's not my place to tell you what to do, I'm just thinking of your own comfort and well-being."

"I appreciate it," said the lemming, and he shook his head in disbelief. He was actually feeling guilty about having offending an eight-foot boa constrictor. Offending it by calling it a snake. The lemming sat down where he was, and tried to sort things out once again. It seemed as if in the past few days reality had been turned upside down and inside out, not once but several times, and he wondered if it continued doing so whether he'd eventually end up where he started. A horrible thought. He yearned for some simple companionship. An exchange about the weather. Something boring and pleasant that had no ultimate meaning.

The snake emitted a groan and twirled off into the woods, returning shortly afterward with another stick, which got deposited once again on the woodpile.

"You're gathering wood," said the lemming, surely a statement that couldn't be misinterpreted.

"I am," said the snake.

"Do you work for the bear too?" the lemming asked, taking things a step further.

"No, I don't work *for* him, I work *toward* him," the snake said pointedly.

"Oh, yes," said the lemming, nodding sagely. They were back to square one.

"I don't mean to be arbitrary," said the snake, "but there's an important distinction. Things need to be done around here and we all do them."

"If you don't mind my saying so, gathering wood seems like the wrong job for you."

"What do you suggest I do?" asked the snake.

The lemming tried to think of something constructive that a snake could do but nothing came to mind. "You could at least find something a little less abrasive, couldn't you?" he said finally, "This line of work seems to be chewing you all up."

"The abrasiveness comes from the rolling, not the gathering," said the snake.

"Then why don't you move in your regular way?"

"What way is that?" asked the snake.

"Your usual way," said the lemming, afraid to say anything that might suggest reptile.

"You mean *slither?*" the snake said pointedly.

"Yes, the regular way."

"I don't do that anymore," the snake said with finality.

"Why not?"

"I'm done with all of that," the snake said curtly. "I'm involved in something else right now."

"It's probably none of my business," said the lemming, "but it doesn't look as if it's doing you much good."

"You mean the rolling?"

"Whatever it is you're involved in," said the lemming. "Look at you. You're all chewed up. You're in very bad physical condition."

"I don't care about that," said the snake.

"You don't care that you're a mass of bruises and cuts and dents?"

"No, not really."

"How can you say that?"

"I don't think about it," said the snake. "My mind is on other things." He rolled over slowly, emitting a painful groan, and began to head back into the woods in his peculiar fashion. "More wood," he said weakly as he rolled off.

"Do you want some help?" the lemming asked. "You look like you could use a hand."

"I could use two hands and a couple of feet," said the snake.

"I didn't mean it that way," said the lemming fearful that he might have said the wrong thing again.

"It's true," said the snake, "I could use two hands and a couple of feet."

"Well, we could all use something," said the lemming, as he joined the snake in his search for fallen branches. "True enough," said the snake. "We could all use something." He put a stick in his mouth, rolled a few feet with it, thought better of it and stretched out on his back again. "I'm just going to take it easy here for a few minutes. You don't mind, do you? I'm actually in a tremendous amount of pain."

"Please," said the lemming, "take a rest. I can do this."

With a long sigh, the snake closed his eyes, stretched himself out straight, and propped his head against a fallen branch. The lemming took a long look at him. There was something trustworthy about this snake, he decided, something direct and comfortable. Vulnerable, too, he had to admit, with his two yards of unprotected stomach sticking straight up in the air. Not what he would have expected from his first encounter with a reptile. *"Who would have thought?"* he said to himself, shaking his head. Paradoxes within paradoxes. Perhaps the snake would give him a straight answer about what went on here, if he could only formulate a question that demanded one. The snake was obviously connected to the bear in some way. The nature of the connection was not clear, but there was a connection. "I work toward him," the snake had said, whatever that meant. *"Toward* him. Not *for* him." Word games. Everyone here played word games.

"Listen," said the lemming. "I'd like to ask you a serious question."

"Shoot," said the snake.

"What is this place?"

"What place?"

"This place. The clearing."

"It's just that. It's a clearing."

"What I mean is, what goes on here?"

"I don't know what you're talking about."

"I'll tell you what I'm talking about," said the lemming. "I was minding my own business, dying quietly under some dry leaves, which was fine with me. Then I get grabbed up by a huge cat who tells me that a bear has some business with me. Then when I get here the bear proceeds to tell me my whole life story in intimate detail. Then he asks me what I want, and he hypnotizes me or something, and I start telling him very personal things. Things you don't often say to strangers. Stuff I might have *thought* about, but not things I would have said. Or even believed, if you know what I mean. And anyway, if he knew my whole life story, he'd also know what I want, wouldn't he? If he could actually read my mind (which I don't really believe he did) but if he *could* then the rest would be easy, wouldn't it?" the lemming looked over at the snake for help. "Am I making any sense?" he asked, quite sure that he hadn't.

The snake was all attention; his head was raised, and focused tightly on each word of the lemming's.

"It's all very simple," he said, cutting through all the confusion.

"I'm happy to hear it," said the lemming.

"You're looking for your lion. That's why you're here, that's why we're all here."

"I'm not looking for my lion."

"Hear me out," said the snake forcefully. "You asked me a question. Do you want to hear the answer?"

"I do, yes. With all my heart."

"All right then, listen," said the snake. "None of this is real," he went on, making a sweeping gesture with his head.

"None of what?" asked the lemming, bewildered.

"This," said the snake. "This stuff around you."

The lemming knew immediately that he was in serious trouble. "What is it then, if it's not real?"

"Let me speak," said the snake. "It's a figment of our imaginations. We manufacture it to keep from finding our lions, which is what life is all about. But since no one has the courage to face that fact, except the bear, who is himself a lion. Everyone goes around behaving as if this is reality. But the bear, out of his great compassion, helps those of us who have found our way to him, so that we too may know ourselves as lions."

"Fascinating," said the lemming.

"Yes, it is," said the snake.

"It's more or less what the duck was telling me."

"Oh, yes?" asked the snake in alarm, "She told you all this, did she?"

"Pretty much," said the lemming.

"What else did she tell you?"

"That was about it," said the lemming. "She just kind of intimated that she was a lion."

"I don't believe it," said the snake painfully.

"What's wrong with that?" asked the lemming. "I thought that was the idea?"

"It *is* the idea," said the snake, "but Marion tends to get a little carried away."

"Then she isn't a lion?"

"I don't know what she is. If she says she's a lion, then she's a lion. Who am I to question the wisdom of a duck?"

"You don't sound like you mean it."

The snake squirmed painfully. "She gets dramatic. She gets grandiose. She says things she shouldn't say."

"That presents kind of a problem, then, doesn't it?" said the lemming. "How do we know when someone has found their lion? I mean, what if I went around saying that I was a lion? That I'd found mine? What would happen?"

"You'd be lying."

"Yes, but who would know?"

"*You* would know. And the bear would know."

"That's true, provided of course that he is in fact a lion."

"He's a lion, all right."

"How do you know? How can you be sure? The duck says she's a lion, and you don't seem to believe it."

"I can't be *positive* he's a lion," said the snake, "only when I am a lion myself will I know for sure that he's a lion. But I *do* know that he's not a bear."

"What's not a bear about him? He looks like a bear, he lives in a cave, he lumbers around. He's a bear!"

"He's not a bear."

"That's fine to say, but how do you know?"

"I *see* him. I *know* him. There are things about him that separate him from the rest of us. Take my word for it."

"Like what."

"He spits birds."

"So what?"

"*He spits birds! Think* about it. Mice rest in his armpits. Think of what it *means.*"

"Mice rest in his armpits?" the lemming asked incredulously.

"That's right."

"That I didn't see."

"Well, they do," said the snake. "Take my word for it. What do you suppose it means?"

"It could mean fifty different things."

"Name three."

"It could mean—" The lemming couldn't come up with any significance to mice resting in a bear's armpits. "I don't know what it means," he said.

"There. You see?" said the snake smugly.

"Well, what *does* it mean?" the lemming asked, getting slightly desperate for some simple clarity. Everything seemed to be slipping into oblivion again.

The snake looked very intently at the lemming. "It means that there is a comfort about him. A warmth. An energy. Bluebirds want to rest in his mouth. Think of it. It's a kind of miracle. It's safe in there. Don't you understand? Do you know what it means to have birds feel safe inside a bear's mouth?"

"It's very interesting, there's no question about that," said the lemming. "It's a very interesting phenomenon."

"To say the least, my friend, to say the least. And let's not forget the fact that he *knows* things," said the snake. "You found that out already. You said yourself that he knew your entire past. What do you make of that?"

"He knew my past all right, there's no question about that. But that doesn't make him a lion."

"It doesn't make him a bear, either."

"I think we're on dangerous ground here, thinking-wise," said the lemming. "There are plenty of ways he could have found out about my past without being a lion."

"For example?"

"Well, it's not as if my life is so mysterious," said the lemming. "Maybe he has scouts out checking up on things. How do I know?"

"To what end?"

"How do I know?" asked the lemming. "It got me here, didn't it? I'm thinking about staying around, aren't I? Maybe that's the end he has in mind." It was a weak argument, and he knew it. It would have meant the bear keeping a watch on him endlessly for his entire life. Even thinking that way was paranoid coupled with delusions of grandeur, and he was very grateful that the snake didn't point that out to him. "Well, it's all very complicated," he said, hoping to end things for a while. His brain hurt.

"Everything is complicated," said the snake. "But life here in the clearing is less complicated than other things."

"In what way?"

"Well, for example, take your old life. Was that easy to understand? Was any of that comprehensible?"

"Not much of it, I have to admit," said the lemming, "not much of it at all."

"Neither was mine," said the snake.

"How did you come to be here?" asked the lemming.

"It's a long story," said the snake.

"I've got nothing to do," said the lemming.

"Well," the snake began, "I was sitting in the middle of the jungle one day, halfway across the world, minding my own business, and from out of nowhere an eagle pounced on me. I tried to fight him off but at the time I was in a very weakened condition and he was immense. Anyway, he picked me up and carried me off, and we just kept on flying and flying. I couldn't figure out what was going on. For a while I was sure that I'd end up as lunch for his brood, but we never stopped. We went over mountain ranges, oceans, deserts. Anyway, several days later, out of a clear blue sky, he dropped me. He let go. Just like that. For no apparent reason. We were about four miles up at the time and I was sure that it was all over, and I wasn't even upset about it. I must have been numb by that time. I hit the top branches of those big pines over there and bounced from limb to limb all the way down. I was so broken up that I was sure I'd die. I couldn't move for weeks, but then this possum found me and dragged me to the bear. He nursed me back to health, and here I am."

"It's a little like what happened to me," said the lemming.

"It's *exactly* like what happened to you," said the snake adamantly. "Everyone here has the same story. You'd had enough of being a lemming, I'd had enough of being a snake. It's the same for all of us."

"What's wrong with being a snake? I thought you guys had things pretty much under control."

"Some do, some don't," said the snake, fading out of the conversation.

"What happened?" asked the lemming. "I'd like very much to hear about it."

"I don't want to talk about it," said the snake, squirming uncomfortably. "It's a revolting story."

"I'm not a prude," said the lemming, his curiosity getting the better of him. "It'll be good to talk about it. Get it off your mind."

"It won't work," said the snake.

"Give it a try."

"I *have* tried. It doesn't help."

"Try it again," said the lemming.

The snake sighed painfully and leaned his head back on the log. "Remember, this was your idea," he said.

"Don't worry about me," said the lemming.

"Well, my life was pretty ordinary in the early days I was living in a tree at the edge of a river, this was back in the jungle—and things were OK, I guess; I wasn't terribly happy but I didn't know anyone who was, so it wasn't much of an issue. Anyway, I was up there in my tree, brooding about life and things of that nature—and, as happens, I got hungry. Well, boas tend to wait for a while before they do anything about hunger; we kind of let it roll around for a week or two till it becomes serious—and uhh—you don't want to hear this."

"Yes I do," said the lemming.

The snake turned over onto his stomach and continued. "Anyway, this capybara started hanging around—"

"What's a capybara?" asked the lemming.

"Rodent. Big. Bristly. Piggy hair," said the snake. The lemming immediately had a sense of foreboding. That perhaps he shouldn't have pressed the issue.

"Anyway," the snake went on, "this capybara came traipsing by, and I grabbed him and we struggled for a while, but I finally got myself wrapped around him, and did what boa constrictors do, which quieted him down, and then when he stopped moving—" the snake winced. "I can't talk about this any more," he said, and pushed his head beneath some leaves.

The lemming could see what was coming, and the hair was starting to bristle on his neck, but he had to hear the rest. "Go on!" he said. "Finish up. Get it off your chest."

"Well, what can I tell you?" the snake said ruefully. "I ate him. I swallowed him whole. That's what happens, that's what boa constrictors do. Let's face it."

"Ghaaa!" the lemming cried, involuntarily, and nausea started to set in.

"Anyway, I swallowed him, and when he was halfway down a terrible thing happened. I heard him calling out. I heard crying coming from inside my own self. In my hunger I'd neglected to crush the life out of him, and the thing was alive! It had needs. It had feelings!"

"Oh, my God," the lemming gasped, clutching the earth with all four extremities so as not to fall off. "Oh, my God!" He had heard enough, but the snake kept on going.

"And our relationship at that moment was so close, that his feelings became my feelings. His thoughts, my thoughts. And it filled me with a horror past your ability to imagine. I went into a kind of shock and then a terrible revulsion set in."

"Oh, God," the lemming moaned, with a paw to his mouth.

"Well, what could I do?" the snake went on. "I spat him up like a geyser and watched him run off into the jungle."

"Oh, God!" cried the lemming, "Oh, my God!"

"Yes," said the snake, "*Oh, my God* is right. He was fine. But my life was ruined. Hunting and trapping became impossible. Every time I tried to bag something, I'd hear the sound of that capybara yelling inside me and I'd run off in terror. Survival became a serious issue, because I couldn't eat anything. I tried dead things, but they made me sick. I tried nuts and berries with the same result, so I ended up on a diet of weeds and ferns, which I could just barely survive on. But nothing, nothing at all would stop the nightmares. It was hell on earth, let me tell you."

"Oh, God!" called out the lemming, who had turned completely green.

"And these waves of self-loathing just kept coming and coming," the snake went on, completely caught up in his story, "I had terrible feelings of guilt and alienation—torment and misery, and the screams of that capybara echoing endlessly in my brain. I couldn't face my own people, I couldn't face myself, I couldn't do anything. I prayed to die so I could stop myself from thinking. And then the eagle carried me off. At the time I thought it would be a fitting end to a bizarre and wasted life."

"Oh, God," cried the lemming again, gasping for breath, "That's a really terrible story."

"It was your idea," said the snake.

"You were talking about a *rodent*, for God's sake!"

"I can't help it," said the snake, "that's what happened."

"I'm a rodent," said the lemming, "how am I supposed to feel now?"

"*I lived it,*" said the snake, "you just had to hear about it."

"I know, I know," said the lemming. He held up a paw to ward off anything else being disclosed.

"Does it sound familiar?" asked the snake pointedly.

"No!" protested the lemming, "how could it?" He began some deep breathing to clear his head.

"It's the same as your story."

"Are you crazy?" the lemming said, "You eat my relatives and you tell me our stories are the same?"

"Forget the details for a minute," protested the snake.

"Details? You think swallowing my family members whole is a detail?"

"What's the matter with you?" asked the snake with great annoyance. "Can't you be *objective* for a second? Can't you just listen to someone for a minute? I'm trying to make a point here!"

"Sorry," said the lemming, making an effort to pull himself together. "You know you don't hear a story like that every day."

"Will you listen to me, for God's sake?" said the snake.

"Yes, sorry," said the lemming.

"What I'm trying to say is that everyone thinks their case is different. You were a misfit as a lemming. You were a failure. Then you got spirited away by a cougar. It's the same story."

"Well, there are similarities, I admit," said the lemming.

"It's the same story," said the snake.

"On one level," said the lemming, "not on another."

CHAPTER 7

It was the best morning of the lemming's life. Not a stick was gathered. Occasionally he would use one as a baton to try and conduct the lengthy discussion, but that was the extent of it. All work was abandoned. And the subjects covered were endless. Life, death, strength, weakness, music, humor, nature—nothing was left out, and before the morning was over, the instinctive fear he felt for reptiles had vanished, and the lemming knew that he had found a friend. The snake's name was Russell, it turned out, which the lemming felt to be oddly fitting. "An interesting coincidence," is how he put it, but the snake was unimpressed.

"Everything is a coincidence," he said.

"I don't believe that's true," said the lemming.

"Why not?" asked the snake.

"Well, *coincidence*," the lemming explained, "that means two events joined together in a strange and provocative manner. Two things happening at the same time in a way that makes you doubt your sanity. Something like that. It's as if for a moment the whole universe is playing a joke on you."

"That's true enough," said Russell, "but who's to say when those two events take place? Who decides when things cross each other? Maybe incidents bang together all the time and no one notices. For example, being a boa constrictor and having Russell as a name seems like an interesting coincidence if you think my mother grabbed the name out of a hat. But what you don't realize is that half the boa constrictors in the jungle are named Russell. And that makes it no longer a coincidence, but just something that is."

"Half the boa constrictors in the jungle are named Russell?" the lemming asked incredulously.

"No," said Russell. "It was just an example."

"But don't you see?" shouted the lemming passionately, waving his stick. "Don't you see what an incredible coincidence it would be if half the boa constrictors in the jungle *were* named Russell?"

"Yes," said Russell, "It would be. Unless someone intentionally sat down and said, "Snakes make a rustling noise when moving through grass and leaves, therefore we will name half of them Russell. Then it would no longer be a coincidence."

"True," said the lemming.

"But what I'm driving at," Russell said, "is that practically everything is a coincidence. For example, two blind birds not flying into each other would be a wonderful coincidence. A boulder falls from a cliff, and you're forty miles away and never even hear about it. That's another good one."

"I see your point," said the lemming. "Three friends having lunch. What about that?"

"Yes," said Russell, "a fine coincidence."

"Or waking up and finding out that it's morning?"

"One of the biggest," said Russell.

"I've got it now," said the lemming.

"The thing is," said Russell, "when you look around you and see how delicately and subtly everything hangs together, how dependent one living thing is on all other things, and how with all the fear and stupidity and selfishness that exists in the world things keep on going at all—why that's the biggest coincidence that I can think of."

The lemming was enraptured at this idea. His mind was spinning with new thoughts, new concepts. They were the kind of ideas he'd had sometimes when he was alone, but not to be taken seriously, and nothing he'd ever dare mention to another living soul. He would have been laughed at and ridiculed. Then a look of confusion came over his face.

"What is it?" Russell asked, "What's wrong?"

"I don't know," said the lemming, "Everything is terrific until I think of this lion business. I can't fit that in anywhere."

"Give it some time," said Russell.

"Is it an idea of something that's so subtle it can't be put into words?" the lemming asked. "Is that what it is?"

The snake shook his head. "No," he said, "the lion is a reality and when you find him you find yourself, and everything in the universe becomes clear."

The lemming mused painfully on the idea. "I would like that to be true," he said. "I would like that very much."

"Why do you look so unhappy when you say it?" asked the snake.

"I don't know," said the lemming uncomfortably. "It makes too much sense, if you know what I mean. *Nothing* makes that much sense. It's too easy. It's against nature."

"Give it some time," said Russell.

CHAPTER 8

They were too late for lunch. Everything had been cleaned up and put away, so they helped themselves to a few quick mouthfuls of corn and a couple of fiddlehead ferns and went to the farm for the afternoon. The lemming had never seen a farm before, and it was like a miracle to him. He'd heard stories about them, farms owned by certain insects in obscure parts of the world, ants and the like, but here was one right in front of his eyes. Rows and rows of familiar things that he'd had to search frantically for all his life grouped together in an orderly and friendly pattern, and the simplicity of the idea, the practicality of it, was wonderful to him. The control it gave over one's own life was too much to even contemplate. And like all great and simple ideas, it was right beneath the surface of his mind. He chided himself for not having thought of it himself. If not him, then some other lemming should have come up with this idea instead of wasting their lives with endless random foraging, gossiping, and fighting among themselves. If in the entire history of his people there had been one moment of silence, or peace, or of order, *someone* would have thought of it.

Marion, along with her numerous other duties, was the farm supervisor, and at the moment she was poking orderly holes in the earth with her beak dropping seeds in the holes, and then with her wide feet she stamped around on the dirt to cover up the seeds. The lemming volunteered his services, and Marion put him to work pulling out plants that had decided of their own volition to live next to the ones she'd put in. He went at the work enthusiastically and with too much speed, but after pulling out some of Marion's new plants, and getting a couple of scoldings, he slowed down and paid more attention to what he was doing. The rows of plantings were too narrow for Russell to roll between, so he busied himself getting rid of the stones and debris that had been thrown to the periphery of the garden, carrying off each little thing one at a time, moaning and groaning with every move he made.

The day was very hot, and the lemming's job, sensible as it was, became slightly tedious after a while. It was a type of work that he had never experienced. He'd never had to do the same thing over and over again, and it started doing strange things to his mind. His initial reaction was restlessness, then boredom, and then in the middle of the boredom a kind of rhythm set in. The rhythm began to feel interesting, adding a kind of relaxed power to the monotony, and after a while the rhythm began to do the job all by itself. All he had to do was keep out of the way. Then for the briefest of moments, he forgot who he was. It was an electric moment. He jumped involuntarily, and shook himself back into the present. Strange, he thought. It had been very pleasant. Very relaxing. Why was he frightened? To have forgotten that he was a lemming for even that brief moment was exactly what he'd hoped to do, and yet he had just done it, and it had frightened him. Why is that? he asked himself. Hard to answer that one. What a mysterious thing is the mind. Perhaps the problem was that he didn't believe anything lived underneath the lemming. He knew he didn't believe there was a lion beneath his short brown fur, but he thought he believed *something* lived in there. Perhaps he didn't. Well, he said, to comfort himself, better to be an unhappy lemming than nothing at all. Or was it? Should he dare to take the plunge and see if something was actually there? Let the rhythm take his mind away from himself long enough so that the thing inside him (if there was a thing inside him) could make itself known? But what if the thing within him was something horrible and twisted that once released, turned on him and devoured him. Or worse, what if it was a void? An empty nothingness going on into infinity? He shook his head vigorously to rid himself of these strange thoughts. Ways of thinking he'd never touched on before. Were they crazy thoughts, he wondered, or only the result of not running so fast? Maybe they were the thoughts shared by all creatures whose lives consisted of other things besides running and fear. Maybe that's what hawks thought about when they were drifting about effortlessly on a current of air.

A terrible noise starting coming out of Marion. It whipped the lemming out of his reverie, and he turned to see if she had been taken ill suddenly. But she was still happily poking her holes and stamping her feet. What was she doing? Surely it couldn't be singing. It was too horrible for that, even for a duck. He listened further, and he decided that it had to be her version of the hum. Tuneless, monotonous, nasal; vibrating everything loose in the vicinity, it was a pitiful imitation of what the bear had been doing in his cave. There was no doubt about it, the duck was trying to shake her brains loose, and the attempt seemed a bit superfluous. Her brains were loose already. Any more humming and they would spill right out of her head. "Quu—a—ack!" she went, "Quu—aaa—ck!!" over and over again, and before long the lemming began wishing that his own brains would shake loose so as not to have to listen to her anymore. He tried to work as far away from her as possible, but there was no escape. Her horn blew at the same volume no matter which direction she was pointing. He tried to stuff beans in his ears to block out the sound, but her piercing wail worked its way right past them. The noise went right through his brain and worked its way into the pit of his stomach. She'd find her lion all right, he thought, but not in the way she hoped. Any self-respecting lion would have silenced her already for what she was doing.

As a last resort he tried to block her out with the sound of his own voice. He started singing to himself and ran through every song he knew, but it was only moderately helpful, so he began a sort of hum of his own in retaliation. When his voice neared her pitch and vibration, oddly it began to wipe out the effects of her honking. Why was that? he wondered. His own voice mixed with hers turned her sound into something else. It wasn't as if what he was doing was so beautiful, but when he added his drone to her honk it filled up the cracks in her sound, took off the rough edges and blended it into something bearable. Interesting concept, he thought, as his brain started to rattle. What should he call it? The law of sympathetic vibration, perhaps. Filling in the insanity cracks. Something like that. He promised himself to think more about that idea when the sun wasn't baking his body to a crisp and his back didn't ache from the position he was in, and his brain was screwed down a little more tightly in his head.

CHAPTER 9

There were two new faces at dinner. A shy possum named Ida with an inscrutable smile, and Gwen, an exquisite doe, who stayed by herself on the periphery of the clearing, watching and listening to everything that was said, but participating not at all. When anyone caught her eye, she'd prance nervously for a moment, and then turn away. There was an invisible wall around her that said, "Don't touch."

It was the possum's job to feed Russell, which was one of the strangest things the lemming had ever seen. The possum had Russell cradled in her lap, or as much of him as she could gather up, and she spooned soup into him as if he were a baby. It was an odd picture, to say the least, and it gave the lemming a few moments of concern about his new friend. He longed to yell out, "What's going on here? Why don't you just eat regular?" But they were so relaxed and unselfconscious about it, that he thought better of it. "Keep still and learn." he admonished himself. "Sooner or later something will become clear." He'd try to keep an open mind, as he had promised Russell. After all, it took all kinds, didn't it? In the meantime, as much as it was possible, he tried to look at other things.

"What do they call you, anyway?" asked the bear over his last mouthful of soup. It was the first time during the meal that the bear had spoken, and the broken silence caused the lemming to jump.

"Excuse me?" asked the lemming, shaking himself out of his reverie.

"What's your name? What do they call you?"

"I'm called Bubber," said the lemming.

"Oh, yes," said the bear, "Bubber. That's what your sister called you before she was able to say Brother."

"That's correct."

"But it's not your name."

"No," said the lemming, "My real name is Herman, but I never cared much for it."

"Interesting," said the bear. "Very portentous."

"How so?" asked the lemming.

"Think about it," said the bear. "Herman in Spanish, means 'brother.' At any rate, *hermano* means 'brother,' which is the same thing as Herman, isn't it? *Hermano* and Herman."

"Almost," said the lemming.

"It is," said the bear. "It's the same thing. Except for the "o" in *hermano* it's the same word. So you have a good situation regarding your name. Your real name means "brother," and you were called "brother." Did you ever stop to think what that might mean?"

"No, I can't say that I have," said the lemming.

"Think about it," said the bear. "Everything points to brother. Since that's what we're all supposed to end up: brothers, or brothers and sisters, you're pointed in exactly the right direction." He drifted off for a while, lost in the beauty of the words and symbols, then he snapped back. And the *"O"* he said with urgency, "let's not forget about the *"o"*."

"Ah, yes!" said Russell. "The "o" in *hermano!*"

"*Right,*" said the bear, "the 'o' in *hermano*. What do we have there?"

"The perfect letter," said Russell.

"Yes," said the bear, "the perfect letter. Within the 'o' you will find all things." He drew a big "O" in the air with his paw.

Everyone nodded some more, pondering the name of the lemming and the letter 'o,' and then it became quiet again. The lemming started to feel that perhaps they were waiting for him to make some sort of comment, so he said, "That's good to know."

"Yes, it is," said the bear. "It's very good indeed. So, we will call you Bubber." he said, slapping himself on the knee, "What do you think about that?"

"Sounds good to me," said the lemming.

"It's quite a responsibility, you know," said the bear gravely, "your name is your target. It's something to live up to."

"I can handle it," said the lemming.

"I'm sure you can," said the bear. He nodded happily to himself, lost for a while in a vision of names and letters and responsibilities, shook himself back into the present and wandered back into his cave.

Russell, Marion, and Ida watched the bear lumber off into the darkness, love and admiration written all over their faces. Russell shook his head in disbelief. "Something, eh?" he said to Bubber.

"Yes, it's something, all right," Bubber answered.

"And now you have your name," said Russell.

"What do you mean?" asked Bubber. "I always had my name."

"Not true," said Russell. "When the bear names you, you have your name. Until then it's a mixed bag. Mistakes made by parents. Limitations and accidents. But when the bear names you it's an arrow into the future."

"He didn't do anything," said Bubber. "He named me the name I already have."

"He *sanctioned* the name you already have. That's the same as giving you a name."

"In what way?"

"Well, it could have gone a different way entirely," said Russell. "You could have ended up being called Charles. Morton. Anything."

They were off again, and there were no footholds. For a while in the morning there had been a solid place to stand, but it was all over now.

"What's wrong with our regular names?" Bubber asked.

"As it turns out there's nothing wrong with them," said Russell. "We're all very fortunate. Our destinies have been a through line taking us from the moment that we were born, right up to this point. It could have been otherwise."

"No, it couldn't," said Bubber.

"Yes, it could," said Russell.

"How could it be otherwise!" Bubber shouted. "How could anything be different from the way it turned out! This is it! This is what happened!"

"From where you stand you're completely correct," said Russell, "but just consider for a minute that perhaps you're standing in the wrong place. Stand somewhere else for a while, and while you're there, all I ask is that you concede the possibility, just the *possibility* that there is more to reality than you are capable of seeing right now."

Bubber started to say something and then he took a good look at the snake in front of him, bruised and dented and twisted and bent, soup dripping from his mouth, lying like an infant in the arms of a possum, and he began to laugh. "My God," he thought, "we're all crazy."

"What's so funny?" Russell asked.

Bubber looked for a way to explain, but there wasn't any. A drop of soup had fallen from Russell's chin and was resting like a small lake in Ida's stomach. When Bubber saw this he grabbed his stomach and rolled around on the ground and started laughed like a maniac.

"What's funny?" Russell said again, not at all amused.

"Life!" Bubber screamed. "Life is a riot, Russell!"

"What's funny about it?" asked Russell, anxious to continue the discussion.

Bubber almost choked at this one. His face was now covered with dirt and dust, and a long piece of straw was hanging loosely from his nose. Russell tried desperately to hang onto some decorum, but Bubber's appearance made it impossible. "You look ridiculous," he said scornfully.

"That's a good one, Russell!" Bubber yelled at the top of his lungs. "That's the funniest thing I ever heard!" He was laughing so hard now that it was getting painful, a cramp was developing in his stomach and tears were streaming down his face, and Russell began to go.

"Stop that now," said Marion, trying to calm things down, which sent Bubber into a full hysterical fit, and in spite of himself Russell laughed even louder and his vibrating started tickling Ida and she began to chuckle demurely. Her stomach jumped up and down and it made Russell's head bounce around, and he slid right off her lap. This was painful, and he yelped, and Bubber screamed so hard that he almost retched. The cramp in his stomach had him doubled over in agony, but he couldn't stop laughing. He was in such intense pain now that it set Marion honking, and so loud that it frightened Ida, which made Russell laugh even louder. Then Ida fell over on her head, which drove Bubber completely crazy. They all rolled around on the ground banging into each other and spitting up dirt, and grabbing their stomachs, which were cramped in terrible spasm. All three of them were in an agony of strangled laughter, tears streaming in troughs down their dirty faces, and accompanied by Marion's dreadful honking.

When it finally subsided, they were all too exhausted to move, so they stayed there looking up at the stars, and then they drifted off to sleep right where they were. Bubber was the last to doze off, and he looked around at the motley family that he had fallen into. They were insane here, he thought. All of them. But he loved them. If this was the only purpose for being at the clearing, it was good enough. He looked over at the great pine that he had leaned against the day before, and he felt a need to be beneath it again, so he moved over to it and curled up in the needles that it had kindly dropped for him to use as a bed. "Let this all be real," he said to the tree. "Let it be true. There is no other place for me. The meanings here are fragile. I'm not sure if there are any at all. But there is a reaching for something, and there is a kindness here. If this is not the place for me, then I fear that there is no place for me at all. Please let this be real."

CHAPTER 10

And so it was that Bubber came to stay at the clearing. How long he would remain there he didn't know. He had no real belief that a lion lived within him, and if he even thought about it for any length of time the idea became completely absurd, anxieties would begin to beset him, and he'd start questioning the sanity of everyone and everything at the clearing. So he tried to the best of his ability to keep away from these dark nooks and crannies of his mind. In his best moments he could rest in the idea that he was having a good time here, and if everyone was insane it didn't matter much. These other pathways were dead-ends, creating more fear and solving nothing. He also knew that since there was nowhere else to go he'd best show some respect for the beliefs shared by this small band of misfits that had become his family. On the occasions that he was able to clear his mind of doubts and fears, he threw himself into the life of the clearing with great vigor. And in doing so he found that his days had an intensity to them that he had not believed possible. He was often frustrated, often confused, but he was never bored and never lonely and his values were constantly challenged. More would happen in one hour at the clearing than took place in months during his life among the lemmings. And whether or not a lion was the end result of all his work, most of the time it didn't matter terribly much. Other miracles were taking place. There they were, mammals, birds, and snakes, strug-gling, sweating laughing together, enjoying each other's company most of the time, and surely this was unique in the animal kingdom. There was some fighting occasionally, some jockeying for position, some petulance, to be sure, but there was a bond that held them together and it was much deeper than their small differences. The nature of the bond was not clear to Bubber, since he wasn't particularly looking for his lion, but the bear said that when those parts of his mind that were clogged with lemming were loosened and spat out, there would be room for "cosmic lion wisdom" and he would understand things easily that were now too much for his tiny mind. Things like the nature of the bond he shared with the others at the clearing.

A serious problem for Bubber was that the bear wasn't around much. He stayed in his cave or grumbled around in the middle of the night or showed up for an occasional meal, but at these times he didn't want to talk about Bubber's problems with the universe. If he did talk at all, it would usually be about the soup and why one ingredient was right and one was wrong, why some things should only be eaten in the morning and others in the afternoon, and why the hum should be done while cooking. These discussions didn't interest Bubber at all. He found that they had no bearing on his problems with the nature of existence. And the nature of existence didn't seem to interest the bear much. Whenever Bubber would tentatively ask a question that related to life's deeper meaning, the bear would begin a hum or drift off into his dream state, which seemed suspiciously like sleep to Bubber, although everyone insisted that he was deeply into his lion at these times, and that it was a great honor to see the bear in this condition. Bubber stayed on the fence about all this, and tried to keep away from all lion discussions as much as possible. Once, in a moment of weakness he confessed to the bear that he didn't believe he had a lion inside him, and the bear answered, "Do you think he cares?"

he didn't believe he had a lion inside him, and the bear answered, "Do you think he cares?"

Then there was the fear that there *was* a lion inside him. Once in a while when he had nothing else to worry about he would say to himself, "If I work very hard on myself, and allow this lion to emerge and fulfill his destiny, what will become of the me that is Bubber? Where will I go? Will I shrivel up and die? Am I just food for the lion to munch on? Like the albumin in egg?" This was yet another disturbing line of thought, and one nobody seemed anxious to help him with. The bear, who supposedly knew these things, didn't talk. Everyone else (who by their own admission had not become lions) was happy to talk endlessly about these things, spouting theories and quoting endless sources, but with no firsthand knowledge.

"I felt something in me once," Marion said. "I felt the lion stirring in me. Trying to get out."

"How do you know it was the lion?" Bubber asked.

"I just know it was. It was like nothing I'd ever experienced before," said Marion. "It was a feeling of great heat inside me, and I felt as if I would pass out."

"I've had that many times myself," said Bubber. "I call it heartburn and acid indigestion."

"You don't understand anything," said Marion.

"True," said Bubber.

"Don't be so proud of it," said Marion.

"I'm not," said Bubber.

"Yes, you are," said Marion. "You think if you keep saying you don't understand things enough times, it shows how intelligent you are."

"I'm not!" Bubber protested vehemently. "I really don't understand anything at all!"

"I know," said Marion, "and you should keep quiet about it too."

Although he put up a good front, Bubber was hurt by her statement and he put it on the endless list of things that he would bring up with the bear if he ever had a minute alone with him.

Bubber was just beginning to reconcile himself to the idea that nothing would ever be made clear, that he would spend the rest of his life talking endlessly about things he knew absolutely nothing about, when, one morning Marion announced that she had the most wonderful news. The bear was going to give a lecture on the meaning of life. It was something he did periodically when his energy was full, and the occasions were always a cause for great joy and celebration. There would be many preparations too, for although public announcements were never made, the word always got out, and visitors would arrive from all over the countryside.

"This will be good," Russell said to Bubber gleefully. If he had paws, he would have rubbed them together. "Now you'll find out what it's all about. We'll get down to some basics."

"And not a moment too soon," said Bubber, with his hopes high for a change.

Everyone immediately threw themselves into cleaning, decorating, and gathering food for the event. It was a difficult task, too, because there was no real way of knowing who would appear and what individual diets would consist of, so Marion, who took charge of such events, would always plan the broadest possible menu, and then hope for the best. They all went out searching for an endless array of berries and nuts, edible roots and ferns, pieces of bark and flowers, mosses and buds, shoots and tubers. Russell and Bubber often went out together, as did Marion and Ida. Occasionally when they were feeling happy and positive they would go out as a group. As usual, Gwen was cooperative and polite, but always silent, always aloof. On the rare occasions when she did speak, it would be something curt and barely audible. It was depressing being around her. Particularly now, when things were so hopeful and festive. Bubber's energy was so high that in frustration at one point he went right up to her and clapped her on the flank. "How about the lecture, Gwen? What do you think? We'll know what it's all about now, won't we?" Gwen just tossed her head, whispered a few words under her breath, and trotted off. Bubber shook his head in dismay. Someday he'd get a rise out her, he thought. Some kind of enthusiasm for something. Some sense that she was a member of this group.

"What's eating her?" Bubber asked Russell, greatly annoyed by her lack of participation, "Why is she so hoity-toity?"

"I don't know," Russell answered, "Some secret pain she's burdened with. Everyone who ends up here seems to have something stuck in their throat they can't get down, something they can't deal with."

"She acts like she's the only one in the world with problems," said Bubber.

"Well, it's probably gnawing at her so much that she can't see what anyone else is carrying around. Give her time. Be a little compassionate."

Bubber tried to find compassion for Gwen, but it was difficult. He looked for her pain, but all he could see was superiority and snobbishness.

"Keep working on it," Russell said. "Compassion is very important."

Bubber thought that was probably true, and wondered if Russell had any compassion for Marion.

"I don't think compassion is what she needs," said Russell.

"What does Marion need?" Bubber asked.

"What Marion needs is a fast kick in the rear end."

"What good would that do?" asked Bubber, slightly alarmed at Russell's aggressive attitude.

"It would shake her up a little bit," said Russell. "Make her think."

"Yes," said Bubber, "But not about the things you want her to be thinking about. She'd just think you were nuts. And anyway, what about *her* pain?"

Russell thought about that for a while and decided that Marion's pain wasn't very interesting, and that anyway some folks needed compassion and some needed a fast kick in the rear end.

"Who decides?" Bubber asked. "Who decides who gets which?" But Russell didn't answer him.

Bubber enjoyed gathering nuts and berries for the big event, and he worked more hours on it than was needed. He looked forward to the bear's lecture with great anticipation, and hoped fervently that what ever was said would help to get rid of some of his fears and doubts and confusions. Since he arrived at the clearing, he'd been happier than ever before in his life. There was no question about that. But he didn't trust it. If he thought too much about anything, he'd start to feel that the underlying ideas around here didn't hold a lot of water. After all. Lions inside? How could anyone believe such a thing? The idea was completely removed from anything practical and solid. From any rational viewpoint, it didn't make sense. And yet, as absurd as the idea was, when he was alone he would sometimes pretend that it was true, just to see what it might feel like. He would strut around with his chest all puffed out, and sometimes he'd even try a growl or two, the way he imagined a lion would growl. A couple of times he even tried purring, which sounded suspiciously like the bear's hum, and he began to think that the hum was perhaps nothing more than an attempt to imitate a lion, but Russell told him that it wasn't true. That the hum had nothing to do with purring. He also said that Bubber didn't have to imitate a lion to become one.

"Just get rid of what you are, and then the lion will spring forth fully formed of its own volition."

"That may be true," said Bubber, "but if I imitate

him a lot, I'll be used to him when he comes out and the shock won't kill me."

Most of the time the bear was in his cave now, and sometimes his hum would thunder through the clearing, causing things to spill and fall over, and Bubber would wonder what he could be doing for so long all by himself in the dark. Bears hibernate, it's true, but the bear didn't do that anymore (being a lion), and there was enough sound emanating from the cave even when he wasn't humming to let everyone know that he was up and busy. But what he was busy with was anyone's guess. It turned out that it was a question on everyone's mind, but for some reason or other no one had ever asked him.

CHAPTER 11

The day of the lecture finally came, and the first guest to arrive was A. J. Turner, a huge vulture, with a shy and unassuming manner who, very early in life, had gone into revolt at what other vultures referred to as food. Even as a child he had felt that the habits of his people were morbid and filthy, and when he brought it up with his family he was laughed at and mocked. So early one morning he left home, only to discover that the other animals of the world were not terribly eager for his company. There was nothing dangerous about him, or unclean, or even unkind, but in his presence most creatures seemed to become highly conscious of their final destiny, and for this reason he became outcast. In addition, his diet didn't really agree with him. It caused his bright scarlet head to peel and flake and created a constant snowstorm on him and everyone around him. He was not unaware of the effect his appearance had on others; he was used to the gasps that his presence caused, and since he was shy by nature anyway, over the years he became deeply apologetic about just being visible. But at the clearing he always knew he was welcome. He would return to see these dear friends several times a year. Ida and Marion constantly nagged him to stay, but his need to be alone, and his curiosity about the nature of things drove him into a life of traveling. He had just returned from a seminar given by a group of dolphins called "Life as Dance," and he spent half the morning of his arrival telling everyone about the wonderful things they were doing in that field. In his shy way he was a wonderful storyteller and often held everyone enthralled with tales of what was going on in the world.

Soon after his arrival came the small birds. A noisy group of sparrows and chickadees. They came in shifts, a few at a time, and then flew right off again, pretending that they were there only for a rest on their way someplace else. They were filled with themselves, and wouldn't even acknowledge their hosts at the clearing. A. J. Turner looked up at the chattering birds and shook his head sadly.

"Look at them," he said. "They're only here for the excitement. They don't want to hear about the meaning of life, they just want to pick up some gossip so they can run off and titilate some other brainless chatterers. They don't intend for it to effect them in any way. What they don't understand is that the lecture will only be exciting if we're intent on doing the work that the lecture will only hint at. We arrive at the meaning of life thourgh effort and struggle. In fact, I think perhaps that is the meaning of life. I hope not, but maybe it is. In any case, I look forward to hearing the bear speak, because I know this: if life does have a meaning, he has found it."

"How do you know?" Bubber asked.

"His struggle is over," said A. J. "He just *is*. He's the only creature I know that simply *is*."

Bubber didn't see that as yet, but he said nothing.

A loud flapping of wings announced the arrival of a group of crows. Unlike the smaller birds, they remained silent, stationing themselves like sentinels in the trees above, intently watching over everything. Bubber had a great affection for the crows, and he smiled when he saw them. He examined them longingly, hoping that he might see an old and cherished friend among them, but he could not find his face. A family of foxes arrived soon after the crows. Mother, Father, and four beautiful cubs, all of them interested in everyone and everything, laughing appreciatively in all the right places—and then all of a sudden Cougar came into the clearing, all swagger and bluff and accompanied by two unpleasant-looking badgers. Cougar stationed himself on the periphery of the clearing, proud and aloof, and the badgers headed right for the food. They took enormous helpings of everything, ate nonstop, and dropped food everywhere. Ida and Marion followed around picking up after them, mumbling under their breath, and trying hard to behave themselves.

"What's all the grumbling about?" Russell asked.

"Look at them," Marion answered. "Badgers. They don't have any interest in the bear, or the meaning of life either. They've just come for the food."

"Well, maybe they'll find out the meanng of life anyway, whether they want to or not," said Russell.

"It would serve them right, wouldn't it?" Marion snorted. "And what about Romo over there?" she asked surreptitiously. "What does he want?"

Russell looked over at the cougar. "He wants something to poke holes in. Whatever the bear says, Romo will find a way to prove him wrong. Wait and see."

"Can't we be friendly for a minute, for crying out loud?" Bubber complained, tired of all the sniping. "It's a social gathering. Let's be social." He headed over to Cougar to make him feel welcome. "Hello there," he said warmly. "Nice to see you."

Cougar nodded curtly.

"Can I get you something to eat?" Bubber asked, rubbing his paws together, "Some fern paté? A little acorn mousse?"

Cougar gave Bubber a long, knowing look, and a secretive smile crossed his face. Bubber started to back away, but Cougar restrained him with a paw. "So!" he said, pulling gently on his whiskers, "I gather that the bear wanted to see you after all! It seems that once I left, whatever business you two had to transact got taken care of."

"Not exactly," said Bubber.

"Well, you're still here, aren't you?"

"I am. I'm still here. There's no question about that."

"Which seems to indicate that he wanted something, doesn't it?" said Cougar. "Or would you call that a wild assumption?"

"It's not a wild assumption," said Bubber. "It's a long story, and I'm not sure this is the time for it."

"I'm here to discover the meaning of life," said Cougar innocently. "Any help you can give me in that direction would be greatly appreciated."

"I think that's the bear's department," said Bubber.

"He's not here yet," said Cougar. "A few private introductory remarks wouldn't upset the apple cart, would they?"

"I'm just here to learn," said Bubber. "I'm not really the one to talk to."

"What have you learned?" asked Cougar.

"Well," said Bubber tentatively, "mostly about lions. Do you know about lions?"

The cougar looked at Bubber for a long time in innocent surprise. "Do I know about lions?" he asked finally. "Yes, I do. A little. I am a lion after all—yes, I know something about lions."

"No," said Bubber, hastily shaking his paws, "I know you're a lion. I don't mean your kind of lion. I mean the kind of lion you have inside, if you get my meaning." It was too late to stop now. He hoped someone would call him away with urgent business. Cougar nodded patiently, waiting for him to finish. "You know about that, I assume," Bubber went on. "You know about the lion you have inside."

"Yes, I do," said Cougar, as if he were talking to an idiot. "I know about the lion I have inside me."

"Well, we all have that inside us," said Bubber.

"Oh, I hardly think so," said Cougar.

"Yes, we do. According to the bear we have lions inside us, and our work is to get them out."

"Really!" said Cougar incredulously.

"That's what I'm told," said Bubber.

"Who's told you all this? The bear?" asked Cougar. "Is this his conception?"

"No, he hasn't told me much of anything yet," said Bubber. "I've hardly seen him since I've been here."

"Do you go around telling everyone these stories?" asked Cougar.

"No," said Bubber.

"That's probably wise," said Cougar.

"You asked me what I've learned," said Bubber.

"So I did," said the cougar. "But this goes more under the heading of gossip. Wouldn't you say?"

"Perhaps so," said Bubber, leaning toward the gathering as if in a stiff wind.

"Why haven't you seen the bear?" asked Cougar. "Has he been away?"

"No, he just keeps to himself a lot. He mostly stays in his cave."

"Doing what?"

"Well, he does the hum for one thing—do you know about the hum?"

"Yes, I do."

"Well, he does that—he does the hum—other things as well."

"Like what?"

"Like shuffling around—humming—other things."

"And you get satisfaction out of all this?" said Cougar. "Some sense of deep fulfillment?"

"I feel pretty good here," said Bubber, "I made some friends . . . I like the food, the air's good . . . I don't know if that explains much."

"No, no, it explains a lot," said Cougar, his voice filled with implications. "Thank you for all this."

The humming in the cave stopped, and Bubber breathed a sigh of relief. "Something's happening," he said. "I'd better go now."

"I'll talk to you later," said Cougar. Everyone rushed to put away their food and find seats. There was some excited whispering and coughing . . . and then the bear came out of his cave. He walked slowly to the center of the clearing, stood up on his hind legs and, with his paws held high and a look of great joy on his face, he saluted all his friends at the clearing. And then in a slow and deliberate tone he started to speak. "A squirrel was once gathering nuts on a mountain top," he said. "A few of the nuts rested on the very edge. As the squirrel went to pick them up, the ground gave way beneath his feet, and he went plummeting off the side of the mountain. Many thousands of feet below, a wren of his acquaintance was making a nest in the side of the same mountain, and as he was smoothing a circle of straw he happened to look up and see the squirrel dropping past him at an enormous rate of speed.

"Morgan, is that you?" the wren called out to his friend.

"It's me, all right," said the squirrel as he fell out of sight.

"How are you doing, Morgan?" called the bird.

"So far, so good!" shouted the squirrel in reply. "So far, so good!"

A hush fell over the crowd. Everyone stared intently at the bear, waiting for him to continue, but he just stood there, with his arms outstretched, looking over his audience with an expectant smile on his face. No one moved, and the silence grew long and painful. One of the badgers coughed. A bird sighed. The bear turned away and walked back into his cave.

For what seemed like an eternity the perplexed gathering sat in respectful silence, waiting for some hint of what to do, for some explanation what was going on. The foxes exchanged furtive glances, and one of the badgers swaggered over to Marion. "What's happening?" he said, "when does the lecture start?" Marion mumbled something incoherent and changed her position, trying to give the impression that she was lost in thought. Bubber looked questioningly at his friends to see what he should be feeling, but no one gave him a signal. Russell was on his back gazing blankly at the sky, A. J. was inspecting his feet, Gwen was her usual impassive self, and Ida was smiling at thin air. As the silence got thicker, Bubber sidled over to Marion. "What's going on?" he whispered.

"I don't know anything," said Marion.

"Was that it? Was that the whole lecture?"

"I don't know anything," Marion snapped. "I'm sitting here. The same as you."

"What do we tell everyone? We have guests here from all over the place. We have to say something."

"We don't have to do anything at all. They came here of their own free will. No one forced them. Plus which they came to hear the bear, and they heard him."

"Maybe we should sing some songs or something," said Bubber.

"You'll do nothing of the kind," said Marion. "This isn't your party, it's the bear's. If he wanted singing, he would have sung something."

Cougar wandered over to Marion, a big smile on his face.

"Well!" he said, "Quite some doings!"

"Hello, Romo," said Marion, casually smoothing down her feathers. "How are you?"

"So far, so good, eh?" said the cougar gleefully, "I was way out in the flats. Over on the other side of the mountain, busy with some important matters, but the word came down to me that the bear was finally going to open up a little. Share some of the good news. Let the cat out of the bag, so to speak. Well, now, I couldn't miss that, could I?"

"Don't be so sure he hasn't," said Marion.

"You mean he was being cryptic? Obtuse and parabolic?" Cougar said in a loud stage whisper.

"I don't know what he was doing, but I won't find

out by dismissing it. I *knew* you were going to do this the minute you showed up. You didn't come here to learn anything. You came here to rip things apart!" Marion's voice started to rise, and the whole gathering held their breath. She was after all a duck, and Romo was a cougar, but the distinction didn't faze Marion.

"Keep your voice down," said Romo. "I don't have to take this from you."

"Yes, you do," said Marion. "If you intend to stay here and make a mockery of my bear, you'll take it and take it plenty!"

Cougar gave a short laugh, shook his head, and walked away. "Come on, boys," he called out to the badgers, "let's go and ruminate on the lecture. And find some brains somewhere. We really have our work cut out for us."

The badgers ran quickly to the food, gathered up as much as they could carry, and left quickly with the cougar. Before anyone had noticed, the small birds had left too, and in no time had forgotten that they were ever there. There had been no excitement, no anecdotes to spread around, so the event was useless to them. The crows followed soon after, and then the family of foxes took their leave, but not before telling everyone what a wonderful time they had, how illuminating the talk had been, and how much material they had to work on. They were charming and warm, yet Bubber had the sense that there was less in their amiability than met the eye. Before long all the guests had gone home except for A. J. Turner and an old porcupine who had been asleep for the whole day. Marion flopped down on the ground in a state of exhaustion while Bubber and Ida quietly began clearing up the enormous mess.

"This was the worst day of my life," said Marion, flat on her back, a wing covering her face. "I don't know if I could live through another experience like this."

"It wasn't too bad," said Russell. "It'll take some

sorting out, but there's grist for the mill there. Bear doesn't do things arbitrarily, we all know that."

"Yes," said Ida, "it *was* nice to see some of the old faces."

Russell looked daggers at Ida but said nothing.

"He could have warned me," said Marion. "A two-minute talk didn't need five days of preparation, now did it? We could have done with a bit less sweeping, a bit less cooking, and a great deal less hysteria." She got up and began putting things away with a vengeance. Slamming down food containers and boxes. Ida rushed to help her, and Gwen began gathering up the pine bough decorations.

"The hysteria was your idea," said Russell. "We could have done without that even if the bear had given a three-hour lecture."

"I'm an emotional type," said Marion defensively.

"So we've noticed," said Russell.

"Things mean a lot to me, and I like to be prepared. Is that so terrible?"

"No, it's not terrible," said Russell, "just unnecessary."

"It's not your job to say what's necessary and what isn't necessary," said Marion, tearfully. "Look at you. Rolling around everywhere, cutting yourself to ribbons. Who has the pleasure of dressing your wounds year in and year out? Talk about unnecessary."

"Let's not get personal here," said Russell.

"Why is it alright for you to get personal and not anyone else?" Marion said with a wail. "*Everything* is personal."

"Alright, alright," said Russell, "I'll back off a little. I'll keep my mouth shut. Here." He bit off some leaves and offered them to Marion.

"Thank you," she said, and she wiped her eyes and her beak.

"Feeling better?" Russell asked cheerily, and Marion nodded. "Good," said Russell. "Now if we can stop all the emotionalism, maybe we can try to figure out what the bear meant. It *is* understood that he meant something, isn't it? We all know that he never does anything arbitrarily, don't we?" There was no answer. "Don't we?" Russell asked, more urgently.

"I don't know what he does and what he doesn't do," said Bubber, a bit let down by the events of the day.

"Well, he doesn't," said Russell, "Nothing is arbitrary. Take my word for it."

"I take your word that you believe it."

"What is that supposed to mean?" Russell asked.

"Maybe we'd better talk about it in the morning," said Bubber.

"I think we should talk now," said Russell.

"You talk about it now, and I'll talk about it in the morning," said Bubber.

"May I say something?" A. J. asked quietly.

"Sure," said Russell.

"I don't really feel as if I have the right to interpret the bear," said A. J., "but whatever else he intended, I think the lecture was also a way of his finding how we get along with each other. If that's the case, then we've all failed miserably. One of the things we're supposed to learn on the path of the lion is how to be at peace with our brothers and sisters. If we try to do just that much, perhaps then we'll get to the deeper roots of the bear's meaning. So instead of reacting emotionally and in fear, which really defeats getting at the meat of the lecture, let's just talk peacefully and lovingly among ourselves, and see what we come up with."

"Thank you, A. J., that was very wise," said Marion. "I think we all owe A. J. a vote of thanks."

Russell held himself in check. He didn't need Marion to tell him when to thank someone, but he tried with all his might to find the beautiful place in her that the thought came from, and while the others were being polite he mumbled something vaguely thankful.

"What do you suppose he meant?" Bubber asked A. J., when the thank you's were all out of the way.

"I don't have any answers," said A. J.

"Well, let's analyze it," said Russell. "Squirrels. What about squirrels?"

"In what way?" asked Marion.

"What are they? What do they stand for?"

"Noise," said Ida. "Mess."

"That's true," said Russell, trying to stay positive, "Very good, Ida. They never keep quiet. Frantic. Argumentative."

"Maybe that's it," said Ida.

"What?" Russell asked.

"Maybe he meant if you run around all the time and talk too much you'll fall off a cliff or so."

"That doesn't sound right," said Bubber.

"Why not?" asked Ida.

"Because he didn't seem to mind falling off the cliff."

"How can you tell?" Ida asked.

"Because he said, 'So far, so good.' If he minded, he would have said something else."

"How could he not mind falling off a cliff?" Ida asked.

"That's the thing we're supposed to find out," said Bubber. They sat in silence, brows furrowed, all looking into the earth, as if the answer would spring up like a flower.

"Flight?" asked Russell. "Flying? Something about being airborne? Did he think he could fly? Is that it?"

"I don't think so," said Marion. "He just sounds dense to me. Why didn't he scream for help? Perhaps the bird would have helped him. Caught him or something. He was too self-sufficient. Too smug. That's what was wrong with him."

"The bird couldn't have caught him," said Russell.

"How do you know?" Marion asked.

"He said it was a wren. A wren couldn't catch a squirrel. If he wanted us to believe the squirrel could get caught, he would have made it another bird. Something bigger."

"Maybe it was a true story or so," said Ida.

"So what?" asked Russell.

"Well, if it was a true story, then it had to be a wren," said Ida.

"It doesn't make any difference whether it's a true story or not," said Bubber. "The lesson would be the same."

"True," said Russell. "Let's go back to the beginning. A squirrel is gathering nuts. He sees one on the edge of a cliff. He grabs at it and falls off."

"Look before you leap," said Ida.

"He didn't leap," said Bubber. "He fell."

"Maybe it's several messages," said Russell. "Maybe he was using one story to tell us a lot of different things."

"I think that's true in a way," said A. J. "If you are desirous of learning, then you will gather wisdom from everything you see. Everything you hear. I think Russell is right in that regard."

"But then the bear could have said anything and called it a lecture," said Bubber.

"Yes, I think that's also true," said A. J. "But having some knowledge of the bear, I don't think he did that. I think he meant to teach us one specific thing." They sat waiting for A. J. to go on.

"I think that what the bear is telling us is that we must learn to believe that wherever we are on our journey it's good. That we must stay positive and hopeful no matter what our lives appear to be on the surface. No matter how precarious our situation is, there's always the possibility of salvation. If we stay positive and cheerful and open, our lions will determine the best possible outcome for us."

"He could have fallen into some leaves," said Ida.

"Exactly," said A. J., "or grabbed onto a tree branch, or he could have simply trusted in his lion having a solution to the dilemma that his squirrel couldn't know. But it seems as if he did have that trust, doesn't it? 'So far, so good,' is what the squirrel said. 'So far, so good.' I think that what the bear is telling us is that where we are on our journey is good. Wherever we may happen to be. So far, so good."

They sat in silence, each in their own way thinking of A. J.'s words, and his wisdom and clarity, and how limited their own view of the bear, and how much work they all had to do.

CHAPTER 12

Marion had difficulty sleeping that night. A. J.'s words were inspirational, but the fight with Russell left her depressed and filled with a feeling of failure. She loved Russell, and she respected him, and couldn't understand why every conversation turned into an argument, every greeting a challenge. It disturbed her greatly, and she would sometimes ask the bear what to do about it.

"Don't fight anymore," the bear would say. "Just stop fighting."

"I don't fight," Marion would say, "I never started a fight in my life. You know how I am; I want peace and harmony. But if he says something stupid, I have to say *something*, don't I?"

"No," the bear would answer. "Let him win."

A difficult instruction. Marion tried to do as she was told, but when the chips were down she couldn't keep still. And on the rare occasion when she did manage to keep quiet, she'd carry on an argument with him in her mind. There she would always win. For in her mind she could say things that she would not dare to say out loud.

"I have no past," she would say, "I have shed it. Like you shed your skin. What there is of me is lion. More than you. More than you will ever know." Did she in fact believe that? No one knew. No one dared test her too far, either. For there was something fragile beneath the brash security she presented, and her constant instructing in the ways of the lion. And all in the clearing instinctively felt that it would be better to suffer her well-meaning lectures and abrasiveness than crack her delicate shell. No, she was not a lion, she knew that. She did not know if she would ever be a lion. She did not, in fact, even know or care whether there was any truth in the words of the bear. The idea of it, the romance, the drama kept her occupied and excited, and kept her heart from breaking. And most important, the gentle warmth of the bear kept her from seeking her own end.

She wanted to tell Russell her story. She wanted him to know of her promise, her pain, her beauty. She wanted him to see how intelligent she was, and to love her for it, even if her wisdom didn't follow his orderly and rigid track. She wanted to tell everyone. It burned in her. But she kept silent about the most important part of herself, for fear that if she opened the dam nothing would stop the flow, and then there would be nothing left of her.

Her life with the flock had been grand. As with the lemming, she had felt somehow different. She felt she saw colors more vividly than the others in her flock. She needed to know things that didn't interest them. But unlike the lemming, her parents had taken great pride in her vitality and energy. They would encourage her curiosity and interest in everything. When it came time to mate, they found Gareth for her, a quiet, steady duck who, like them, was content to bathe in her radiance. Marion at first found Gareth boring, but as time went on, she discovered in him a patient, loving nature that became in itself a source of instruction for her. She would flare up and down, feeling sometimes great elation, sometimes great depression, and Gareth's quiet determination and steady strength slowly became her anchor, her security, and her comfort. As all couples in her flock, they became inseparable. But in the case of Gareth and Marion it was more than instinct, it was deep and abiding love. At first it was of great importance to Marion that Gareth join her in all of her discoveries, and he tried with all his might to share her enthusiasms, see what she saw, feel what she felt; but as much as he tried, his system was just not as finely tuned as hers, and he ended up simply enjoying the mystery of her, and recognizing that there was a part of her that he would never know. It made him love her even more. In the early days she would resent Gareth for not accompanying her everywhere. But as time went on she came to be excited by their short separations, because when they were reunited, she found that there was even more to share.

Then on their third season together, as they were flying south for the winter, something caught her eye on the ground far below. The brightest thing she had ever seen. In her usual fashion, she started to fly toward it immediately.

"Where are you going?" called Gareth.

"I have to look at that thing down there," Marion answered. "That thing that's shining."

"It's nothing, Marion, let it go."

"I just want to take a quick look," she called out. "I'll catch up with you in a minute!" She left the flock and headed straight for the light, which was coming from an area populated by man; not the safest place in the world for her to be, but she knew she'd be gone from there in a minute. As she got closer to the light she saw that it was nothing but a huge microwave tower, all metal boxes and dishes glinting when it caught the sun. Some monstrosity that man had planted among the trees. She laughed at herself and shook her head and flew back to the flock, but as she gained altitude and looked around, she saw a clear and empty sky. The flock was nowhere to be seen. "Where could they be?" she thought, trying not to panic. "I was gone only seconds—less than a minute." She flew in higher and wider circles to get a broader view, but there was no sign of her large family anywhere in the sky. She began flapping wildly in every direction, checking the ground to see if they'd landed somewhere for water, or a rest; she darted in and out of the scant clouds, quacking at the top of her lungs, but they had vanished. In a panic now, and flying in jagged circles, she flew blindly into some telephone wires, tore her wing, and fell like a broken kite to the ground. She lay there dazed for a time and then painfully tried to resume the search for her flock, her family, her beloved Gareth, her other half, but they were gone now, into a vacuum, a piece of her broken off.

Shot at, attacked by large dogs, she escaped to a secluded lake and huddled at its edge until she had some mobility and a semblance of health.

A crow began hanging around. At first he made her uncomfortable. He never spoke, but as time went on she began to depend on his visits. One day he flew off, and for no reason that she could understand, she began to follow him. The crow would wait for her patiently when she got tired. When her wing became painful, he would hover nearby or peck at the ground, never speaking or getting too close. Their strange journey continued for many weeks and hundreds of miles, and though she never knew where she was being taken, her secret hope was that it was back to her flock and to her beloved husband. Instead she found herself at the clearing, with the crow gone as silently as he'd come. Here she had remained, trusting the destiny that brought her here, honoring and serving the bear, hoping to see herself some day as the promised lion, and missing her other half with all her heart and soul.

CHAPTER 13

Marion, Ida, Russell, and Gwen spent each morning working on the farm. They would wake themselves at the crack of dawn, shake the sleep from their minds and bodies, eat a scant breakfast, and then coughing and yawning and stumbling into each other, head off to tend the farm. Bubber would watch their early-hour zeal with amazement. "Do you want any help?" he'd yell each morning as they left.

"Only if you feel like it!" Marion would call back dutifully, but since he never did, they'd see him again when they came back for lunch. But after a few days Bubber began feeling a bit guilty about not sharing in the workload. He tried to shake off the guilt, preferring to stay warm and disoriented, but it persisted, so slowly and grudgingly he began gravitating toward the farm. At first it was just for short visits, then he started bringing snacks and something to drink, and before long he was working there on a daily basis, although he continued to have mixed feelings about farming as a full-time occupation. The eating part he enjoyed very much. That was a constant. The other parts of the activity were more difficult to love. Digging for hours in the dirt was mostly torture for him. While he was doing it, he would have long daydreams about the wonderful things he could be doing with his time, like taking a nap, or wandering around, and then he'd begin to feel resentment at having been forced to do the work. Then sometimes lucidity would strike him on the head, and he'd realize that no one was forcing him to do anything; that he was farming of his own free will; that the resentment he felt was in his own mind, and that daydreaming and wandering around and taking naps wasn't so much fun anyway. And then he would find that he was simply there. Sitting in the nice warm dirt. And his work slowed down, the sun became less hot, his back relaxed, and the weeding and cultivating became almost fun. At these times Marion's interminable humming became almost beautiful. He could sense a serious intention behind the sound, and he could almost feel something loosening inside his brain. Some vestigial part that was heavy and unnecessary and restrictive. These were good times, and Bubber would have been happy to have stayed in that frame of mind forever. But it didn't happen. His mind had other plans for him. Questions such as "Where does all this lead?" would begin to bubble up from some swamp and begin to plague him. Boring, stupid questions, that took him down dark paths and never solved anything or made him feel happy. But after a while he started to recognize this vacillation as a pattern, and he began to see how one simple activity could be made to feel an infinite variety of ways depending on how he chose to think about it.

He was musing this way one morning when Ida rushed up to him breathlessly and said, "The bear wants to see you!"

"What for?" he asked, instantly feeling sure that he must have committed some terrible crime.

"I don't know," said Ida, with an inscrutable smile. "I was walking by the cave or so, and he came out and said, "Where's the lemming?" and I told him, and he said, 'Tell him to come by the cave,' and that's all I know." Bubber thanked Ida, brushed himself off, and scurried to the cave with dark fears crowding in on him. The bear had probably read his mind and knew he hated farming. Knew that he spent more time daydreaming and nagging his brain than he did doing any work. He was going to be told to leave.

When he arrived, the bear was sitting in front of his cave staring off into space. Bubber sat down near the bear waiting for an instruction, and they stayed there in silence for a bit. Then the bear looked up as if seeing the moon suddenly, or a strange imaginary bird. An idea seemed to be formulating in his mind. "Mushrooms," he said mysteriously, and got up and walked into the woods.

"Mushrooms," thought Bubber. He searched for some hidden meaning in the word, but couldn't find any, and not knowing what else to do followed the bear into the woods. The bear moved at an easy pace, humming as he went, allowing Bubber to keep up with him, and after a time they came to a moist and shady glen with mushrooms growing in every nook and cranny. The bear found a great piece of bark and using it as a basket began to pick the mushrooms and toss them in. Bubber watched him carefully, and then hoping that it was the right thing to do, he too started throwing mushrooms into the basket. A million questions crowded his brain, questions he was sure the bear had the answers to, but since he hadn't been asked to speak he remained silent.

"How did you like the lecture?" the bear asked suddenly.

"Which lecture?" Bubber asked, stalling for time. "The one you gave?"

The bear nodded.

"I liked it," said Bubber. "I liked it very much."

"You did, eh? You liked it?"

"Yes, I did. I liked it a lot."

"I'm happy about that," said the Bear. "Very happy indeed. Tell me. Did you like it in its entirety, was it a great wash, or are there some parts that particularly stick out in your mind?"

"No, I liked the whole thing," said Bubber.

"Good, good," said the bear, "Did you like its shades of meaning and subtle thematic development?"

"I did, yes," said Bubber. "I liked all that."

"I'd love to hear your impression of the talk," said the bear, smelling a mushroom, "I haven't gotten a lot of feedback."

The lemming looked closely at the bear for a hint of sarcasm or a shred of disdain, but none was in evidence.

"Well, to tell the truth, I had a little difficulty with it at first, but we had a talk about it later and A. J. pretty well cleared things up."

"He did, eh?"

"Yes."

"What did he say?"

"I don't know if I can remember exactly," said Bubber.

"A general impression will do nicely," said the bear.

Bubber stopped picking mushrooms so he could concentrate on his thoughts. "A. J. said that the lecture meant we should stay positive about things. That we should recognize we are alive and well; that our journeys toward the lion are progressing nicely, and that we should just stay happy and loose. I think that's about it." He looked to the bear for some approval.

"Very interesting," said the bear.

"Was that it?" Bubber asked. "Is that what you meant?"

"No," said the bear.

"Ah," said Bubber.

"It's very good stuff, but it's not what I meant. A. J. often finds more meaning in things than God put there. That's a bit of a problem, you know. He's like the man Aesop bit."

"The man Aesop bit?" asked Bubber.

"Yes," said the bear. "Do you know Aesop?"

"I'm afraid I don't," said Bubber.

"Aesop was a wolf of my acquaintance," said the bear, sitting down and putting the basket to one side, "Very large, very mean-tempered, but I found him amusing. At any rate, one day a human being started hanging around the woods near Aesop's den. An old fellow with a beard so long he kept tripping over it.

And this old fellow would spend his days watching flies and beetles, snakes and water rats, then he'd write down stories about their activities as if that would somehow explain his own life to him. He'd chortle with glee every time some little animal did something to confirm his theories; but most of the time they were just putting on a show for him. He'd come in with a lunch basket full of goodies, and they'd distract him with some piece of entertainment, and then they'd steal his food. Anyway, Aesop got disgusted watching the old man hanging around his territory, trampling over everything, changing life around to fit his own simple-minded view of things. So one day when the man was crouched over, examining some ants and a grasshopper Aesop charged him full speed ahead and bit a large piece out of his backside. The man screamed in pain, and when he turned around to see what had happened, there was Aesop glaring at him with the old man's rear end hanging out of his mouth. 'Go write that in your book!' Aesop yelled, and the old man ran off and never came back."

"That's quite a story," said Bubber.

"It is, isn't it?" said the bear. "And that's what A. J. reminds me of. But don't get me wrong," the bear said very seriously. "I love A. J. very much. He's a kind and sensitive bird. He should just stop knowing so much."

"I think I understand," said Bubber.

"I think you do, too," said the bear.

"May I ask something?" said Bubber.

"You may," said the bear.

"What did the lecture really mean?"

"It was a joke," said the bear. "One of my favorite jokes. And nobody laughed. I looked down and there was a sea of vacant faces staring back at me, faces without a trace of humor in them, or understanding, or love or compassion, and I got very depressed so I didn't give the lecture. But it doesn't matter much. No one wants to know the meaning of life anyway."

"Why do you suppose that is?" Bubber asked.

The bear leaned way down to Bubber and stared in his face. "Because it's too easy. That's why." He sat back and began running his paw aimlessly through the mushrooms. "Everyone wants life to be complicated. They want to chew on it forever, and discuss it endlessly. They want something to argue about, something to play around with, to fight over, something to make them crazy or miserable, but no one wants to know the truth."

"I do," Bubber said quietly. "I want to know the truth."

The bear looked at him sharply. "But you already know it," he said. "You've been told the truth by Marion, you've been told the truth by Russell, you've been told it by A. J., you've felt it pressing on you every day you've spent at the clearing; you've heard it whisper to you in your dreams and you were born with it resounding in each fiber of your being. You knew it with absolute and perfect clarity the day you fell into this earth, and still you insist that it's a mystery. Do you think that it will help if I tell you the truth in a new way, or if I cry and plead for you to believe me, or if I chase after you for the rest of my life with the truth held out like a dose of medicine? Do you think that you will believe it then?"

"I will believe it if you tell it to me," said Bubber. "I know what you say is true. I have no doubt about your wisdom or your sincerity."

"Then I will tell you the truth," said the bear. "Through a series of unfortunate circumstances and bad choices, we in the animal kingdom have allowed ourselves to believe that these strange shapes of ours, these lemming shapes, these snake shapes, these duck shapes are what we really are. That this puny conception is all there is to reality. That this—" he banged his chest with his paw several times "—is what it's all about. It's not true. This is what's true." The bear settled himself inches away from Bubber and, looking deep into his eyes, said, "Within each of us is a lion. And though we run in a million different directions to find peace and happiness, it is this lion that we are desperately trying to find. That and nothing else. It is the lion that we have abandoned, and it is the lion to which we long to return. We try to ignore him, but we can't. He can always be heard, no matter how dimly, and when we try to still his voice, we feel terrible pain, great remorse, and unfathomable loneliness. That, in a nutshell, is the whole story. Why do we trouble about it so much, we of the clearing? It's simple. Those of us who have found our way here have heard the voice of the lion a little louder than our fellows. And our lions, tired of their bondage, are clawing at their cages, eager to be set free." Suddenly the bear stood up on his hind legs. "WE ARE LIONS!" he shouted, with his arms spread wide, and his voice reverberated through the forest silencing the million noises that had filled the morning air. "WE ARE LIONS! That is our beginning and our end! That is our future and that is our past! That is our glory and our promise and our peace! It is the one law! It is the one truth! It is the one joy and the one consolation! It is that which has always been and it is that which will always be!" A bird tried to fly into his mouth but he brushed it away. "There you have it," he said. He lumbered back down on all fours and slowly began gathering mushrooms again. "Does that come as a surprise to you?"

Bubber shook his head.

"No, of course not," said the bear. "but doing something about it is another matter, isn't it?"

"I thought I *was* doing something about it" said Bubber.

"What is it that you are doing?"

"Well, what is anyone doing?" Bubber asked defensively.

"I'm not asking anyone, I'm asking you," said the bear.

"I do my share of work—I try to stay happy—I try

to get along with everyone. Isn't that doing something about it?"

"Gathering your own food and talking philosophy is not becoming a lion."

"But that's what everyone else is doing, too," said Bubber, suddenly fearful that his premonition was true, and that the bear was going to tell him to leave. "We all gather food, and we all talk philosophy. I don't understand what I'm doing that's wrong."

"Are you being brave? Are you being good?"

Bubber thought about his answer carefully. "I don't think I'm being bad, if that's what you mean; I don't know if I'm being brave or not."

"What of your lemming have you shed?"

"I'm trying to shed my lemming every moment of the day. I don't know if I'm doing it so well, but I thought it took time. I thought patience was something that I had to learn along with everything else." Fear started to well up within him, and deep inside, in a place he was only dimly aware of, he knew that the fear meant something was missing from his answers. His words were more a plea for mercy than any explanation of position. And yet he continued to justify himself.

"How do you show your love to your brothers and sisters?" said the bear.

"I try to do it the best I can, all the time."

"How?"

"In different ways."

"What of yourself have you shared with Ida? Or Gwen?"

"Ida and Gwen?" asked Bubber incredulously. "It's impossible to have a coherent conversation with Ida," he said. "You talk to her on one subject, and she answers on another one. She can't keep an idea in her head. To tell you the truth, most of the time I wonder what she's even doing here. If this is a path of courage and strength and sacrifice, I think she's in the wrong place."

"It's also a path of love and devotion," said the bear, "but you're not so interested in those qualities. They are not as impressive as courage and strength. And since all of them are qualities that you are wanting in, you wouldn't notice them in Ida, whose courage and devotion are immaculate. There are things you could well learn from her, but it would require giving up not only more of your lemming, but also some conceptions of courage and strength that have no basis in reality."

Bubber's curiosity was piqued. "Could you tell me a little about her?" he asked. "I surely can't see what you're talking about."

"Ask her yourself," said the bear.

"I'll do that," said Bubber. What the bear said was true. He was bored by Ida, and it never occured to him that she might have anything of interest to say. Because she wasn't brilliant or witty, he hadn't looked for any other qualities in her. Now he'd spend more time with her. While he was at it, he'd swallow his pride and try once more to get a hello out of Gwen. And he'd show a little patience for Marion, too. Things were beginning to swim in front of him now. He could feel himself getting lightheaded. The bear's outline was beginning to blur, and he shook his head to get him back into focus. "I've made some bad mistakes," he acknowledged, trying to keep a foothold in the conversation. "As soon as I get back, I'll try to do something about it." The bear seemed to be shimmering now as if he was under water, and Bubber was turning into a bowl of warm mush. "I'll even try talking more to Gwen," he said. "I doubt if she'll answer me, but maybe I haven't given her a good-enough try."

"That's the idea," said the bear, and he was smiling again. "Keep a journal, too. Write down your thoughts. Keep track of the things you see and hear and feel. After a while a pattern will unfold and you'll begin to see who you are." A breeze was blowing through Bubber and his head had no distinct shape any more. Sounds filled his ears that he had never heard on this earth, and electricity was lighting up the inside of his head and it became very difficult for him to understand the bear's next words.

"Look at these woods," said the bear, and Bubber tried to, but they wouldn't stay still. The magic that the woods had always been took over. Soft living light pulsated through the massive trees, flowing through and sustaining everything. He could hear a thousand sounds from a thousand creatures, each one with a history and a life. "Listen to me!" everything cried out. "Hear my story!" And Bubber knew that each story was crucial. He knew that he could have spent the rest of his life listening to just one of them. And thousands of voices were calling out. "Listen to me!" sang the trees, and the birds, and the frogs. "Hear my story!" called the crickets, and the water in the nearby stream, and the moles, and the snakes, the gnats in the air and the squirrels on the ground. There was no danger here. No dark presence, and Bubber wondered why in all the forest he had wandered through, he had never seen a place such as this. Was it because he was safe here with the bear? Seeing it through his eyes? With his strength? Or was this a special and magic place?

"Look at these woods," the bear said again, and he reached into his left armpit, pulled out a pair of gray mice, and threw them vigorously into a pile of leaves. "The whole forest floor is in a state of ferment and decay. Almost no light reaches the ground. It's dark and damp and murky. The whole floor is composed of dead leaves and fallen trees, and this decay is the food of bugs and worms and parasites that cannot bear the light at all. And into this rot and dampness and darkness these magnificent trees drop their seeds, and the rot hides them and nurtures them and feeds them. Some of them survive the bugs and darkness and reach their arms up through the dirt and the rot. Something in them says that there is more to existence. They find in this decay and the murk the strength to help them rise into the air, and they breathe the air and they see the sunlight. And some of them know that it is theirs to claim for their own, but for others it is too far away, and they lose heart and return to the earth. But some few will reach for it with all their strength, knowing that they can have it for their own. They sink their roots down deeper into the earth, but they turn their thoughts high to the distant light shimmering through the branches of their giant brothers, and they start to grow. As they climb they are bathed by more light, which gives them the strength to grow even taller and faster. Their roots dig deeper and deeper into the ground. Some of them lose heart. They get crowded out. Some find nothing to sink their roots into. Some fall half grown, to begin again as seeds. But some few become these giant sentinels living all their days in the warm, sweet embrace of the sun." He pointed up at the great breathing monoliths and watched them lovingly for awhile. Bubber decided that it was time to crawl into the bear's lap. It struck him as an odd thing to do, but he didn't care. He pushed aside a young chipmunk and curled up in the bear's voluminous warmth. The bear was humming to himself with his eyes closed, and Bubber decided that he was never going to move again for the rest of his life. He would stay in the bear's lap forever, curled up like a baby. His mind was jelly and he had no muscles in his body. That was OK. The bear had used magic on him and turned him into a vegetable, but that was OK too. Everything was OK.

As he lay there, he remembered something very important. It was right on the tip of his mind, and it would explain everything in the universe. To get at it, all he needed to do was nudge it gently into focus, but that was out of the question at the moment. Well, that's OK too, he thought, everything is OK. What would his family think, he wondered, seeing him curled up in a bear's lap? They would probably have laughed at him. Well, that was OK, too.

CHAPTER 14

And so after months of doubt and confusion, Bubber was finally touched by the power of the bear. He wandered around the clearing in an ecstatic state, marveling at everything he heard and saw. At times he attempted to describe what had happened to him, but it wasn't possible. Whenever he tried, the response would be a knowing smile or a patient nod.

"I disappeared!" Bubber would say excitedly. "I actually went into some other place and time and actually merged with the bear or something. I can't explain it very well."

"I know all about it," said Russell.

"I don't think you do," Bubber protested. "I really was in some other state of beinghood. Some other conceptualization of reality."

"Sounds good," said Russell.

"It was unbelievable. Everything is clear now. Everything makes sense. I feel alive for the first time in my life."

"I know all about it," Russell said again.

"No, you don't," Bubber said, vehemently. "If you did, you'd have some zest. Some vim. You'd be walking around with a smile on your face."

Russell nodded. Everyone else nodded. They tried to tell Bubber that they'd all had similar experiences with the bear but he wasn't about to hear it. They couldn't have. He knew they didn't know what he was talking about. If they did, their lives would have all been resolved by now. Finished and perfect. They'd all be as happy as he was. Bearlike. Lionlike. He started giving great hugs to everyone he met. Long, crushing ones, filled with love and one-ness. He looked deep into everyone's eyes, trying to make contact with their truth, with their lion, and he'd feel great sorrow for them when they couldn't meet his gaze. He became a friend to all, whether they liked it or not. He became a lover of the universe. Gwen's coolness even stopped bothering him. The air smelled cleaner, and a drink of water became a profound experience. "Taste this!" he'd say at the spring, "can you taste how perfect and alive and beautiful it is? How it's exactly like what it is? Is it a miracle, or what?"

"Yes, we know all about it," his friends would say, and bite their tongues.

As the bear had suggested, he tried to find out more about his friends in the clearing. Who they had been and where they had come from. Russell had already told him more about himself than he cared to know, so he went on to Gwen, hoping that some sincere interest on his part would open her up a little. But she wouldn't cooperate. She told him very politely that certain things were better not talked about. This of course was very intriguing to Bubber, so he started asking around, but no one knew anything about her. There were strange rumors afloat about her having done something terrible to her family (or perhaps it was the other way around). Russell had heard one thing, Marion something else, and none of it made much sense. He asked some of the animals on the periphery of the group what they knew about her, some of the mice and birds and raccoons that came by occasionally, but all he got from them were conflicting rumors, so he finally stopped asking about her. Everyone he spoke to seemed eager to tell him their own life story, however, and most of them were horrible. Tales of cruelty, loss, and terror came at him from all sides, unasked for, and Bubber began to wonder how anyone survived at all. He tried to question Marion about her own life but she shrugged and said, "There's not much to tell—I was a plain boring duck till I met the bear, and now I'm a lion." Bubber suspected there was probably a little more to it, but something told him not to press the issue. She did tell him Ida's story, though, which she'd heard one day from the bear.

Ida had been the runt of a large litter. Frail, without any natural aggression, there was no expectation that she would live, and no one cared much either. Her mother had too many mouths to feed as it was, and the stragglers had to go the way of the unfit. There was no emotion attached to the idea, it was the way things were.

But Ida would not succumb to the concepts of her parents. She kept herself alive by licking drops of milk from the mouths of her satiated brothers and sisters, and then she'd suck on kernels of grain or grass, and though she remained frail in mind and body, she managed to survive; a source of embarrassment for her family, who considered her presence to be an affront against the laws of nature. Sensing that she wasn't wanted or needed, she took to wandering off for days at a time, content to be alone with her few thoughts and happily taking whatever came her way.

One day she wandered into the clearing, where to her surprise she was treated with respect and love. At first she would only visit occasionally. The attention she received was uncomfortable for her. But she could not keep away, and before long she became a regular visitor to the clearing. In the beginning her family took no notice of her comings and goings. But one day she was seen with the bear, and then again, and it became a further affront to her parents. "What are you doing there?" they demanded. "Nothing," Ida answered. "just sitting quietly." They mistrusted her simple answers, and they disliked her. There was no reason for her to be happy, and the simplicity of her answers meant that she was hiding things. Her presence became more and more uncomfortable. Her existence was a slap in their faces. Her survival an affront to possum law and order, and one day she was simply told to leave. If she wanted to consort with bears, they wouldn't try to stop her, but it would be better if she cleared out and didn't return. Ida left without a word, and went right to the clearing. She never looked back, never complained, and never had an unkind word to say about a soul from her past.

Ida's story was very disturbing to Bubber. Each time he thought of it, he was filled with terrible remorse over the way he'd treated her. The way he'd even thought about her. And he began to realize that if he took the trouble to ask, stories would spill out at him from all over the forest, and it would be impossible, finally, for him to be judgmental or superior to anyone ever again.

His vision was clearing. He was seeing more, hearing more, and to keep track of himself he began to keep a journal, as the bear had suggested. In the beginning, it was only a few minutes at a time. Scratch marks that simply reminded him of important things that took place during the day. But as his eyes opened, more and more became important to him, and before long he was writing down everything. Portraits of his friends, descriptions of what he'd eaten for lunch, confessions, arguments and disagreements, anecdotes—he became the chronicler for all the events at the clearing, and he began to feel that this was the serious mission of his life. And since he had to do an enormous amount of quoting, and could never find the passages he wanted, he devised a system of filing so he could run and find things at a moment's notice. He had sections on biography, one for weather reports, one for recipes, one for his dreams, one for analysis of his dreams, one for analysis of everyone else's dreams. He had a section on complaints and confusions, one for his own poetry, one on folklore, one on hearsay, one on general musing, and a very important one for the most minute details of the bear's activities, because Bubber felt that the world had to know everything about the bear.

Soon Bubber was quoting the journal all the time, correcting everyone's memories and reminding them of things they said, most of which they would have preferred to forget. Nothing was safe from his rapier-like porcupine quill. Slips of the tongue, idle chatter, everything got clarified. Then he began to fall in love with the words themselves and how they could be manipulated to change meaning and tone. Soon he stopped doing his chores and while the others were working on the farm or cooking or cleaning he'd read them long sections from his works. "What do you think of this?" he'd ask Marion.

" 'Wednesday;' " he'd read. " 'A beautiful summer's day filled with warm thoughts and slow dreamy feelings.' "

"Nice," Marion would answer.

"Do you think that captures Wednesday?" Bubber would ask hopefully.

"Right on the nose," Marion would say.

"How about this one now," said Bubber, leafing through scraps of birch bark. "Here's another good one. 'Monday; an angry sky this afternoon. It complained and yelled and then began to cry.' " He looked at Marion for approval. "What do you think?" he asked.

"It's quite wonderful. I don't know what to say."

"Can you see what I'm attempting with it?" Bubber asked.

"I think so," said Marion, and she began to clean the big soup kettle.

"Try and tell me," demanded Bubber.

"You're mixing poetry with weather reports," said Marion, thinking fast.

"Very good," said Bubber. "Very good indeed. What about this, now?" he went on. "This pertains to you. I need your OK on this one." He cleared his throat.

- 108 -

"This is straight reporting, mind you; it will seem a little harsh, stylistically," he said apologetically.

"I don't care," said Marion, from deep inside the cauldron.

" 'The bear comes out of his cave at odd times. There is no predicting his behavior.' I ask Marion, 'Why are his activities so random?' "

" 'They're not,' she answers. 'They follow an exact pattern that you don't understand.' "

" 'Do you?' I ask."

" 'Sometimes,' she answers. I watch her like a hawk. On Monday she sets a place for him at breakfast. He comes out at breakfast. She sets no place at lunch, he doesn't come out at lunch. The next day she sets places at all three meals, he comes out for all three meals. The next day she sets no place for him at all, he doesn't come out at all. I look for a signal between them, don't find any."

" 'Does he tell you when he's going to come out?' I ask. She shakes her head no. 'How do you know when he's going to be there?' I ask.

" 'I just know,' she says."

Bubber put down the bark and peered at Marion inside the cauldron for approval. "What do you think?" he asked.

"It's brilliant," said Marion, upside down, scrubbing away at the bottom of the pot.

"I know, but is it accurate?" asked Bubber.

"Perfect," said Marion, and Bubber went off to see if Russell agreed with Marion's evaluation of the piece.

Evenings he spent alone, going over the day's notes and screaming at the maggots who busily tried to chew up his manuscripts. Then one day out of a clear blue sky, the bear told him to stop. "That's enough of that, now," he said, "No more writing."

"Why not?" asked Bubber in alarm.

"You're making everything too serious," said the bear. "It's boring. I'll have to get Aesop after you."

"But it's my life!" Bubber cried out. "I've found my purpose in life!"

"It's not your life, it's your journal," said the bear. "I told you start a journal to bring order to your life, but you're using your life to bring order to your journal. There's a subtle but very important difference there. Do you get my meaning?"

Bubber nodded sadly. "What should I do?" he asked.

"Something else," said the bear.

Bubber thought about that for a while. "There isn't anything else," he said miserably.

"OK by me," said the bear, and it clearly didn't make much difference to him whether Bubber followed his instructions or not.

Bubber thought long and hard about stopping his life's work. He loved his journal dearly. It was the first thing that he had ever done that he'd loved. But then, if the journal was suppose to bring some order to his life, and the bear said to get rid of it, perhaps it had accomplished its purpose. Perhaps now the journal was only the crystalization of lemming stuff. If he got rid of it, maybe he'd be that much closer to his lion. On the other hand he didn't want to just be knuckling in to authority. Acting like a sheep. Fearful of what would happen to him if he didn't do as he was told. He pondered this way, back and forth, and neither choice filled him with much joy, but in the end he gathered his precious notes into a huge bundle and threw it off the side of a mountain. He watched the pages scatter to the winds and sat dejectedly once again, not knowing who he was or where he had been. "Nothing makes sense," he murmured under his breath.

"True," said the bear from somewhere behind him. Nothing *does* make sense. And so does everything else."

Bubber missed his journal terribly. He slowly returned to his schedule of work on the farm, but his heart wasn't in it. He had no special identity there, or anywhere else for that matter. There was nothing that he could call his own personal thing. No craft or ability that made him unique. The journal had swept him up. Swallowed him whole and took his mind away from the constant questioning and nagging about who he was and what he was doing. (If he even really existed at all.) And now it was back to drudgery and self-doubt. Or so he thought for a day or two. Once the initial depression was gone, and he gave up his sullenness and feelings of being put upon and abused, he noticed that he was calmer than he had ever been. That his interest in his surroundings were greater. He listened better, he was more compassionate, he noticed things that before the journal had not existed for him. And he had to admit finally that the bear probably had the right idea. Even so, periodically he'd think wistfully of some little thing, some poem or piece of humor, and he'd find himself writing it in the dirt in the middle of cultivating or weeding. And he hoped that someday, he'd at least be allowed to write one short little book. Perhaps *The Sayings and Proverbs of the Bear,* with one little message on each page. Something like "So far so good," or "Nothing makes sense and so does everything else," and other mysterious, provocative ideas. Even though he didn't understand most of them, they were beautiful things to see and hear, and perhaps someone else could get some sense out of them. But with all his wistfulness about what he'd given up, he did come to honestly believe that the whole episode was for the best. There was no lion in evidence as yet, but he began to suspect that there was a bit less lemming.

CHAPTER 15

For days Marion had been restless and preoccupied. She dropped things, muttered to herself, forgot where she was going, snapped at her friends, and left the usually immaculate clearing messy and disordered. And since she was in many ways the hub of activities at the clearing, her mood began to have a terrible effect on everyone.

"What's wrong with Marion?" Bubber asked Ida finally, after suffering a full week of her ill temper.

"I don't know," said Ida.

"Have you ever seen her like this before?"

Ida shook her head no. Since Bubber hadn't had much luck in getting personal with Marion, he wasn't too keen on broaching the subject with her, but after a full week of disorder and bad cooking he decided something had to be done. "Ida!" he called to the possum, who was fertilizing corn, "go and ask Marion what's bothering her." Ida nodded, wiped her paws on her stomach, and dutifully went off to the clearing where Marion was preparing dinner.

"Hello," Ida said cheerily.

"Hello," Marion answered without looking up.

"Everyone wants to know what's bothering you," said Ida, plunging right in.

"The bear's gone," Marion murmured, and she threw some vegetables distractedly into the pot. Several carrots landed on the ground. She picked them up, wiped them off, and threw them back in.

"What do you mean?" Ida asked.

"Just that. The bear's gone. He's not here anymore."

"How do you know?"

"I can tell. I can feel it."

"Where did he go?" Ida asked.

"I don't know."

"How long will he be there?"

"If I don't know where he's gone, how do I know how long he'll be there?" Marion said curtly. Ida hung around for a while hoping for some more information, but none was volunteered, so she went back to the farm.

"She doesn't know where the bear has gone or how long he's going to be there," Ida said.

Russell and Bubber didn't like the sound of the message, so they left the farm to Gwen's care and with Ida went back to the clearing.

"Something troubling you, Marion?" Russell said.

"The bear's gone," said Marion.

"Gone where?"

"I don't know."

"So how do you know he's gone?"

"I can tell. I can feel that he's not here."

"Does anyone else feel that?" Russell asked.

"I don't feel like he's gone," said Bubber.

"Me neither," said Ida, "What about you, Russell?" Russell shook his head no. "What about Gwen?" Ida went on, "Should we ask Gwen what she feels?"

"I don't need Gwen to tell me anything," Marion said curtly. "The bear's gone, and that's all there is to it. Have you seen him? Has anyone seen him in the past week?"

"I haven't, now that you mention it," said Russell, "at least not that I can remember."

"Me neither," said Ida.

"Maybe he's just hanging around in his cave," said Bubber, "he sometimes holes up in there for days at a time, doesn't he?"

"This is different," said Marion. "I know when he's

in his cave, and I know when he's away. I can tell these things." Marion was beginning to tremble visibly.

"Let's not go overboard, now," said Russell. "Let's make sure of our facts here before we get ourselves in a state. "He wouldn't just go away without telling us something."

"He did," said Marion. "He did say something."

"What did he say?"

"He said that he had to go somewhere and that he'd be back soon."

"Well, that's where he is then. He went somewhere and he'll be back soon."

"Yes, but he never gives announcements about things like that, he just does it. He just goes off if he wants to."

"This time he made an announcement," said Bubber.

"You don't understand anything," said Marion, and she started waddling around the clearing, straightening things at random to keep herself occupied. "What's all the excitement about?" said Bubber. "He went for a walk."

"Wednesday!" said Marion. "He went for a walk on Wednesday! Who's seen him since Wednesday?"

They looked around. No one had.

"So there you are," said Marion. "He hasn't come back."

"You don't know that," said Bubber.

"Yes, I do! I know it."

"So, he went for a long walk," said Bubber, "What's the big deal?"

"It's a *week*, Bubber," said Marion. "It's a *week* since we've seen him."

She went back to her cooking, burying herself in the familiar activity to avoid any more confrontation. The bear was gone. She needed no more proof than her own intuition, and she fought back the fear that would engulf her if she thought about it anymore. She could sustain no more loss in her life. There had been enough.

"Let's just find out if he's here or not," said Bubber.

"Good idea," said Ida.

"Why don't we just keep watch in front of the cave. That way when he comes out we'll see him, and that will dispel any fear we have that he might have gone off somewhere."

"What if he doesn't come out of the cave?" asked Ida. "What will we know then?"

Bubber coughed into his paw. "We'll know two things," he said emphatically. "*One,* either he's gone off somewhere; or, *two,* he's in there and he's not coming out."

"That leaves us pretty much where we are now, doesn't it?" asked Russell.

"No, it doesn't," said Bubber. "Now it's conjecture. That way we'll know for sure."

"If you say so," said Russell.

They held a meeting and organized a schedule of who would keep watch when, and Russell was appointed guardian of the cave in official capacity, since he had no trouble in spending long periods of time lying completely still. He stretched himself out in front of the bear's home, confident that he'd soon see him come ambling out, but after two days he began to have the sinking feeling that the cave might be empty of bear.

"Any news?" Bubber asked on one of his many trips to see what was happening.

Russell shook his head. "It doesn't feel as if he's in there."

"Why not?"

"No sounds," said Russell.

"Maybe he's sleeping," said Bubber.

"I don't think so," Russell answered. "There'd still be a moan once in a while, or a snore, but I haven't heard anything. And there's no *feeling* coming from in there either. No warmth, no smell—no essence of bear, if you know what I mean."

"Have you slept since you've been here?" Bubber asked.

"I dozed off once or twice."

"Well, then he could have gone in and out of the cave a dozen times while you were sleeping."

"I don't think so," said Russell. "I would have heard him and woken up. And anyway, I haven't been alone here very much."

"Well, he can be pretty quiet when he wants to be," said Bubber.

"We'll stay a while longer just to make sure," Russell said, and they continued the vigil at the cave. But after four full days of watching and waiting they began to think that Marion's instincts were right.

"He's not in there," said Russell gravely.

"But we're still not sure," said Bubber. "We're still not completely sure he's gone. There ought to be some way of being positive about it."

"Short of going in the actual cave, you mean." said Russell.

"Yes, short of that," said Bubber quickly, "although as a last resort, I don't think he'd mind us taking a look in there."

"I can't go along with you on that," said Russell.

"A quick peek," said Bubber, "just to relieve our minds. In and out."

"Not me," said Russell emphatically.

"It was just a thought," said Bubber, and the subject was closed.

"Why don't we just stand at the mouth of the cave and yell?" said Bubber. "That would get us some action. Provided he's in there."

Russell deliberated on that for a while and thought it was at least worth talking to Marion about. Marion thought it was fine. Since he wasn't in the cave, it certainly wasn't going to disturb him.

"It's just on the off chance, Marion," said Russell. "Just to make sure."

"Suit yourself," she said.

So Russell, Bubber, and Ida lined up at the mouth of the cave and yelled his name. They listened carefully for some response, but after repeated efforts and nothing but echo coming back, they gave up, feeling certain for the first time that he was gone. They came back to the clearing and huddled over the cooking fire and rested there, looking at the flames and saying nothing.

"What next?" Bubber asked, after a while. "What do we do now?"

"What is there to do?" Marion asked dejectedly, without expecting an answer.

"Well, we're sitting here doing nothing," said Bubber anxiously. "Maybe he fell down a ravine or something. Maybe he's been attacked and is lying wounded somewhere and needs help. We're all moping around, and in the meantime he could be in serious trouble."

"Let's go out and search for him," said Bubber. "We'll check out the entire area. "We'll look for signs, and we'll ask everyone we meet if they've seen him or heard about him."

"Good idea," said Russell, happy to have an activity, and the four of them immediately set off to find the bear. They went off in different directions, establishing points to meet during the day. They called out for him as they went, and asked everyone they came across if he'd been seen, but no one had any news. He'd neither been seen nor heard from, and so, at the end of the day, tired and discouraged, they headed home.

It was quiet that evening at the clearing. What discussion they had was in hushed tones. They sat around the fire warming themselves, each lost in their own fantasies. Bubber watched Marion furtively through the evening. She had always seemed to him unshakeable in her belief in the bear. He could do anything, and Marion would find a way to justify it and make it seem reasonable. This walk of his didn't seem to be a big enough reason for her to be so thrown. And her depression was having a very disquieting effect on everyone. Making things worse than they were. It was alright for him to be upset about it, but he didn't feel it was right for Marion. She should know better. He started to say something about it, but then thought better of it. She was in a volatile state, and it might be better to just leave her alone for a while.

"Well, what do we do now?" asked Ida hopefully.

"Beats me," said Bubber. He picked up some pebbles and began tossing them aimlessly at a leaf on the other side of the clearing.

"I guess we just go on the way we've been," said Russell. "What else is there to do?"

"It would have been nice to let us know," said Bubber. "I mean, he's a special case in a lot of ways, but he could have said, 'I'm taking a *long* walk' couldn't he? I mean what would have been wrong with that?"

"Maybe he couldn't say that," Ida murmured.

"He could have said something," said Bubber.

"Maybe he didn't know he'd be away this long," said Russell. "Maybe it's a surprise to him too."

"I thought he knows all these things," said Bubber. "How come he didn't know he was going on a long walk?"

"You don't know what was on his mind," said Russell.

"Well, I'll be honest with you," said Bubber, "He left at a very bad time for me. I was just starting to get somewhere. I gave up my journal and everything. It would have been a lot better for me if he'd stayed around till something sunk in. It wasn't a good time to run off, in my humble opinion."

"That's just a little egocentric, isn't it?" said Russell. "I mean, the world doesn't revolve around when you decide to do a little growing. Things happen."

"A walk doesn't happen. A walk is a decision."

"Well, we just don't know that, do we?"

"Then what *do* we know?" Bubber asked belligerently. "I thought he was the example of what we're all supposed to be growing toward. What if we all started wandering off whenever we felt like it and then never showed up again? What happens to all those important ideas? The ones that are difficult enough to swallow already? Like being lions? Stuff like that? How are we supposed to believe in lions when we don't even know how long a walk is going to take?"

"He said he'd be back soon," said Ida.

"So?" asked Bubber belligerently.

"Well, maybe it's not soon yet."

"Ida," Bubber said, "Believe me, soon is long past over."

"What about acts of God? What about accidents?" said Russell.

"He should know enough to be able to anticipate things like that. Why didn't he say, 'Barring acts of God and accidents, I hope to see you soon.' Something like that?"

"I think our problem here is with the word *soon*," Russell volunteered.

"Not for me," said Bubber. "I have no problem with the word soon. The problem I have is that the bear *said* it, and he didn't *mean* it."

"Well, we don't know that," said Marion, "He may have a different meaning for the word soon than you do."

"Well, then, why didn't he say so? Or use my meaning? Let him use someone else's meaning for a change."

"Maybe he wanted you to learn his meaning," said Marion.

"Marion, let's face it," said Bubber. "A half an hour is soon. Tomorrow morning is soon. Two weeks is no longer soon!"

"I think we're on dangerous ground here," said Russell, trying to cool things down.

"It's ten days," said Marion, "it's exactly ten days since he's been gone."

"It's ten days since you've been *feeling* that he's gone," said Bubber, "and if he is gone nothing is changed. We hardly saw him when he was here anyway. He was in the cave all the time. Once in a while he'd come mumbling out to tell us we're all lions, and then go back in again for days at a time. Well, what's changed? Why is anything different?"

"You have a good head," said Marion. "No one can beat you and Russell when it comes to brains, but you have no hearts and you have no souls."

"Why is that, Marion?" Bubber said sarcastically. "Because we're not acting hysterical like you? If we all went crazy, then would you be happy?"

"The bear wouldn't like this," Ida said quietly.

"No, he wouldn't," said Russell. "He wouldn't like it at all."

Bubber girded himself with great effort and turned formally to Marion. "I apologize," he said gruffly.

"It's alright," said Marion quietly.

"We shall make table legs of our adversities," said Russell under his breath.

"What's that supposed to mean?" asked Bubber.

"It's just something the bear says. Whenever things get particularly difficult, he says, 'We shall make table legs of our adversities.' "

"What does it mean?" asked Bubber.

"I don't know what it means," said Russell. It wasn't a good time for this particular discussion. Russell would have been happy to calm things down, but he didn't know how.

"Why did you say it?" Bubber asked sharply.

"No reason," said Russell, and he rolled off to be by himself.

CHAPTER 16

All his life Cougar had been plagued by depressions that tore him to shreds and left him feeling empty and useless and dead. He could never tell when they were going to come, and there was no rhyme nor reason to what set them off, either. It would invariably be something completely inconsequential. Some nothing. A look from a stranger, a dream that couldn't be remembered, a skipped meal. Whenever he was off guard, whenever he felt too sure of himself or too happy, the depression was there, lurking in the dark ready to leap on him and throw him to the ground. Earlier in his life, when these fits blew over, he was able to forget that he'd ever had them. But as he grew older the depressions became deeper and lasted longer, and they caused such profound despair that he often thought about running headlong into a tree and putting an end to it all. Either that or seek the help of the bear. In many ways he preferred the idea of running into the tree. It would have been much less humiliating. But the thought of the actual collision, the moment of actual impact was distasteful to him, so with his tail between his legs he'd go off to see the bear.

"I can't do anything for you," the bear would say. "You're a cat. You're stuck with it. It will never go away."

"I'll do anything," Cougar would plead.

"No, you won't," the bear would mumble. "You won't do anything." He would start to walk away from Cougar, but Cougar would cry and moan and pull at the bear. "Test me," Cougar would whine, "Give me a great test. I'll prove myself to you."

"Sit still for ten minutes with an empty stomach," the bear said, hoping that would be the end of it.

"You're joking, aren't you?" Cougar said, hanging on the bear's leg to keep him from going into the cave. "That's all I have to do? Then you'll take me in and help me and love me?"

"Just sit still for ten minutes on an empty stomach," Bear repeated.

At first Cougar thought it was an attempt to humiliate him. But after asking the same question many times, and each time getting the same response, he decided to try what the bear had suggested. Over and over again Cougar tried to sit still for ten minutes on an empty stomach, but as soon as he'd settle himself, keening, yearning voices started calling to him from deep inside, making him terribly restless. He'd begin twitching and thumping his tail, and eventually give up in failure after only a minute or two. The test was so picayune, and his inability to pass so frustrating, that he would have temper tantrums, which would bring on new and deeper depressions, so it was a vicious circle for Cougar. Bear would listen to his dramatic displays in the distance, shake his head sadly, and pray that Cougar would leave him alone, once and for all. But when things were going badly, Cougar would always come back and asked the same question, to which he'd receive the same answer.

"I hate that test, Bear," he'd say. "I hate sitting still, you know that. Give me something else to do."

"Like what?" Bear asked.

"Something bigger. Something with some meat on it. I want to know I've done something when it's over."

"In other words," said the bear, "you want a test that you've passed already."

"I don't know what you mean," said Cougar.

"Never mind," said Bear and he tried to walk away again.

"A test! A test! Give me a test!" pleaded Cougar. "Any one you want!"

"Sit still for ten minutes on an empty stomach," the bear repeated.

"Why doesn't anyone else get that test?" Cougar shouted. "Why am I the only one who has to do small things?"

"Everybody has to do everything," said the Bear, and he shook Cougar off and walked into his cave.

So, things being what they were, it was no surprise to Marion, when, once again, tail between his legs, Cougar came creeping into the clearing. His eyes were bloodshot, his nose dry, his coat matted and filthy, and Marion immediately knew the whole story.

"Where is he?" Cougar asked pathetically. "Is he coming out for dinner?"

"Probably not," said Marion. She threw a cautious look at her friends, hoping that they wouldn't tell him too much.

"Just my luck," said Cougar. "Well, I'd better wait around and see. I'll just hang around for a while, if nobody minds." He fell over on his side, panting heavily.

"What's up, Romo?" asked Russell clinically. "What's going on with you?"

"No good," said the cat pathetically. "The head. The head's no good."

"What was that?" Marion called out. "You're incoherent."

"I'm not well," Romo said, a little louder, this time. "I have a thing taking place. Sick."

"Well, go over by the trees then," stormed Marion, "Keep away from us. You don't want to give it to everybody, do you?"

"Sorry," said the cat, and he got up and moved over to the trees. "It's not contagious," he said. "It's the brain. It goes its own way. It wanders off from the rest of me. I'm sick in the head. Dreams." He lay down again and began shivering and moaning, with a glazed look in his eyes.

"What a mess," said Bubber, somewhere between pity and disgust.

"Don't worry about him," Marion said under her breath, "His misery announces the changes in the seasons. He comes on tough and free but he's the most inflexible item I've ever seen in my life. Every time someone gives him a taste of his own medicine, he comes crawling back to the bear as if the universe had collapsed. He doesn't take well to glimpses of his own mortality. Look at him. Death warmed over. Hey, you! Romo!" she shouted. "You want something to eat?"

He shook his head no. "I can't hold anything down. Everything swirls," he said, and he curled up in a ball. "Oh, God, it's good to be here," he said, his voice choking with emotion. "I keep forgetting how peaceful it is, and how kind you all are. I don't know why you all put up with me." He began to weep with deep, silent convulsions. Bubber looked questioningly at Marion, but her gesture with her head told him that she'd heard all this before.

"I'm sick! I'm sick!" Cougar went on. "I can't stand myself. I run from anything good. I don't trust anyone or anything, I'm arrogant, I'm prideful, I'm selfish. What's wrong with me? Can somebody tell me? How did I end up like this?"

Bubber, unable to stand the torment he was watching went over to the cat to try and comfort him. "Just calm down," he said, patting him on the shoulder, "take a nap or something."

"I don't want to take a nap or something," said Cougar.

"You'll feel better when you wake up."

"Look," said the cat, "I know you mean well, but I'd prefer it if you didn't patronize me. Truth is the only thing that will help me. Not sweet talk. Don't do that to me."

"Sorry," said Bubber, "I didn't mean to sound condescending."

- 124 -

"I don't want temporary solutions." said Cougar. "I don't want the easy way out anymore. You were placating me. I can tell that tone. I've done it too often not to recognize it. I know you meant well, but please don't do it any more."

"I was just trying to be nice," said Bubber defensively. "Those are things one says when one is trying to be nice."

"They were generalizations. Old saws. Placebos. They won't help me. Just say what's on your mind. If you don't, I'll go crazy completely."

"Will you stop all that now?" snapped Marion. "You're depressing everyone."

"Sorry," said Cougar, instantly contrite. "I didn't mean what I said, whatever it was. I shouldn't be near anyone. I'll go and wait for the bear." He got up and headed for the cave.

"That's all we need," said Russell, when the cat was out of earshot.

"What do we do now?" asked Ida.

"There's nothing to do," Marion answered. "He'll wait for a while, and when the bear doesn't come out he'll get restless and leave in a huff, like he always does."

"Let's hope so," said Ida.

They waited for Cougar to make some ambiguous impatient noises, but throughout the evening there was nothing but silence from the cat, and after a while they assumed that he'd gotten bored and left. But the next morning as Ida passed the cave on the way to the berry patch, there he was, out in front, resting patiently, head on his paws like a dog. She nodded to him, he grunted back and that was that. Immediately she ran back to inform the others.

"He's still there," she said breathlessly.

"Wonderful," said Marion.

"What should we do?"

"Nothing," said Marion. "We go about our business."

"What if he keeps on hanging around?"

"He won't. He'll get bored and go away like he always does."

"What if he doesn't?"

"What if?" said Marion impatiently. "What if cows had wings?"

"No, but what if he finds out that bear's been gone, or so? What will happen?"

"I don't know anything," said Marion, "I'm sitting here, the same as you."

Late that afternoon Cougar walked over to the farm, where Bubber was cultivating. There was a frown on his face. "I don't think he's there," he said to Bubber, switching his tail nervously back and forth.

"You don't think who's where?" Bubber answered.

"The bear," said Cougar. "I don't think he's in his cave."

"Oh, I think he probably is," said Bubber, trying to keep the inevitable at bay for as long as possible.

"There's no sign of him in there."

"Have you been in there?" Bubber asked with alarm. "Did you go in the cave?"

"No, no," said Cougar. "But there are no sounds from in there, and no smells either. He's not there."

"Oh, I'm pretty sure he is," Bubber said, trying to muster up a smile.

"No, I don't think so," said Cougar, "and what's more, I think he's been gone for some time."

"Well, I think you're wrong there," said Bubber.

"When did you see him last?" Cougar asked.

"Let's see," said Bubber, "When did I see him last?" No answer wanted to come out. "I'd better ask Russell."

"What do you have to ask Russell for?" said Cougar, "I asked you when *you* saw him last. Not Russell."

"Well, we were together when I saw him last," said Bubber and he walked over to Russell.

"He suspects the bear's gone," he whispered. "What should I tell him?"

"How does he know?"

"The same way we all know," said Bubber. "I'm trying to stall him off but it can't last forever. I don't like him hanging around."

"Me neither," said Russell.

"Why don't we just tell him that we don't want him here right now?"

"Fine with me," said Russell, "Who's going to be the one?"

"Hmm—" said Bubber, his thoughts going immediately to Marion. He walked back to Cougar and said, "Russell doesn't remember when he saw Bear last." He mumbled some excuses and ran off to find Marion.

"What do we tell him?" He asked Marion after he'd explained the situation.

"We tell him nothing."

"Well, he's going to get suspicious eventually. We have to tell him something."

"Why?"

"Why? What do you mean why? If we don't tell him something, we'll be stuck with him forever."

"Make up a story then," said Marion, "Tell him whatever you think right."

Bubber ran through a list of things to tell Cougar. "How about this?" he said. "He's gone off to visit his large brother and is coming back here with him."

Marion thought it was swell, and Bubber started off to tell Cougar but the words dried in his throat. It was a good story, and would probably ward off trouble for a while, but someone would confuse it, probably Ida, Cougar would get suspicious, and they'd be in worse shape than they were now.

CHAPTER 17

Cougar padded around restlessly for the whole day. He paced up one pathway, down another, examined the entrance to the cave, munched on everything in sight, and then started all over again. He didn't speak much till that night, but when he came back to the clearing he was fuming. "When's the last time anyone saw the bear around here?" he asked fiercely. It was the question everyone was dreading.

"A few days ago," said Ida.

"How many days ago?"

"What was it, was it five?" Russell asked, pretending to search his memory.

"More like twelve!" Cougar snapped, "Why didn't you tell me he's been gone for a week and a half. You let me hang around here like an idiot, and nobody said anything."

"We didn't know anything definite," Bubber stammered.

"You're lying!" said Cougar. "Every toad and fly in the area knows he's been away. Don't try to play games with me." He padded around looking suspiciously at everyone. "Why are things being kept from me?" He demanded.

"Nothing's being kept from you," Bubber said gently. "We just thought you were upset enough. We could see the state you were in, and we didn't want to make things worse."

"I told you already I don't want to be placated," said Cougar. "I need straight answers."

"Well, we knew about the sweet talk, but we weren't

sure about the placating. Now we know," said Bubber. "It won't happen again. Sorry."

"Where is he, then?" Cougar demanded.

"I think he said something about visiting his large brother," Bubber mumbled, "and then coming back here with him. Did anyone else hear that, or was I the only one?"

"I didn't hear it," said Ida, and Marion and Russell shook their heads no, and that was the end of that." Maybe I got it wrong," said Bubber.

"Has anyone checked inside the cave?" asked Cougar.

"What for?" Russell asked.

"Maybe he's left a note or something."

"We don't go in there," said Marion.

"Why not?" asked Cougar, "if you want to know where he is, that's the first place to look."

"We don't go in there," Marion said again, more forcefully this time.

"Well, I need to see him badly," said Cougar.

"We all need to see him badly," said Marion, ruffling her feathers.

"I need to see him worse than you do!" Cougar bellowed. "Look at me. Look at the state I'm in." He held out a paw, which had a sizable tremor. "What does that tell you?" He said accusingly, "Nobody else has one of these." He rolled over on his back and shoved his paws under his armpits to try and keep them still, and stared petulantly at the sky. "I'm going to hum for his return," he said abruptly.

"Sounds good," said Marion.

"I'm going to do that. I'll sit outside his cave and hum all night. Maybe that will get things going. Maybe I'll have a vision of where he is. Hear voices or something."

Fat chance, thought Marion, Hum all night! He hasn't hummed two minutes in the last five years.

Cougar got up abruptly and padded off to the cave, and everyone breathed a sigh of relief. "That should be the end of him," Russell whispered. "He'll hum for about thirty seconds, get bored, and go about his business."

"Let's hope so," said Marion.

They finished their chores and just as they began to settle down, Cougar's hum filled the evening air. An angry, abrasive, nasal, grinding sound, that set everyone's teeth on edge. "Well, that can't last long," said Marion.

"Let's hope not," said Russell.

But to everyone's surprise, Cougar found the stamina, or fortitude, or faith, or whatever it was to hum without stopping until early the next morning, keeping everyone up in the bargain.

"He's doing the hum, though, isn't he?" said Bubber with a yawn at around four A.M., "I'll say that much for him. He's got more stamina than I do. He's been at it for about seven hours straight, and he's not slowing down either."

"A fine time he's picked," said Marion with her eyes closed.

"Well, growth is growth, whenever it takes place," said Bubber. "You've got to hand it to him."

"Growth is growth and keeping people up all night is keeping people up all night," said Marion.

"What would Bear do with a situation like this?" asked Russell.

"He wouldn't have to do anything," said Marion, "Cougar wouldn't dare to make such a racket if the bear was around."

"But suppose he did. What would the bear do?"

"Who knows?" said Bubber. "Nobody can ever predict what the bear is going to do?"

"Why don't we hum to find out what Bear would do?" said Ida.

"Good idea," said Russell. "If Cougar can hum for his return, we can hum for instructions."

"We should hum for his return too," said Bubber. "If Romo is doing it, we should, too."

"If he's doing it, I don't want to do it," said Marion.

"Yes, but he's humming for a good thing. Why can't we do it too?"

"You do it if you want," said Marion, "I'm not joining him in anything. And anyway, I don't interfere in the bear's life. If he's gone, he's supposed to be gone, and if I hum for him to come back I'll be disrupting his plans. What do *you* think about that, *Gwen?*" she asked fiercely, turning on the deer out of nowhere.

Gwen whirled around as if she'd been hit. "I—I haven't made up my mind yet," she said, and started pawing the ground nervously. It was almost odd to hear her voice, it had been so long since she'd spoken to anyone.

"At any rate, that's how I feel about it," said Marion, turning back to the group. "I don't want to tamper with things."

"You're right," said Russell. "We have to be careful what we hum for. It's not a good idea to disturb the 'what is.' "

"How do we know what's supposed to be and what's not supposed to be?" said Bubber. "I mean, that gets into a very serious discussion, here. If we're not supposed to change things, then we shouldn't hum for anything at all. We should just leave well enough alone."

"What's well enough alone?" asked Marion.

"In what context?" asked Bubber.

"You're the one who brought it up," said Marion.

"Well, it's a lot of different things, isn't it?" asked Bubber.

"My point exactly."

"I'm a little lost here," said Russell. "What's going on?"

"If you know what well enough alone is then leave it!" shouted Marion. "Otherwise, do something else!"

"Look, it's four o'clock in the morning," Russell pleaded. "Can we get into the fine philosophical points at some later time?" And he pushed his head under a rock as far as it would go.

"Here's what we'll do," said Bubber. "We'll hum to see what bear would do. Then we do it."

"Who says we can do what Bear can do?" asked Marion.

"Alright then," said Bubber, with a resigned sigh, "we'll hum to see what Bear would want *us* to do. How about that?"

"Fine," said Marion.

"Is that OK with everyone?" Bubber asked. Everyone murmured yes.

"*How about you, Gwen? Is that all right with you?*" Marion snapped.

"Yes, fine, fine," said Gwen hastily.

"Well, let's hear it once in a while," Marion grumbled.

They sat silently in a circle and waited for someone to start things, and since no one did, Bubber coughed into a paw and began to speak. "To whom it may concern," he said piously, "May this hum shake our brains entirely loose, and in the loosening, may the bear hear our call and tell us what we need to know. Hoping for a speedy reply, and the wisdom to understand it when it comes; if it comes; we remain, affectionately, your friends at the clearing." Bubber quietly began a hum. Then one by one everyone joined in. The bear had suggested on many occasions that they hum together, but this was the first time they ever attempted it. The sound was ragged and diffused at first, but soon it found its own direction and then before long a vibration started between them that felt very similar to the bear's own sound. It was exciting and alarming, and they immediately stopped.

"Anybody get anything?" asked Bubber.

"Not much," said Ida. "I just thought about the bear shaking his head and walking into his cave, or so."

"Not me," said Russell. "I had a vision of bashing Cougar's head in with a rock."

"No help there," said Bubber.

"I thought pretty much what Ida thought," said Marion. "I saw the bear just sitting and staring endlessly at Romo."

"So did I," said Russell.

"No, you didn't," said Marion. "You said you wanted to bash him."

"Not at first," said Russell. "First I saw the bear, but he was just staring at Romo, not doing anything, so I decided to take things into my own hands."

"I saw the same thing," said Bubber. "The bear was watching Cougar to see how long he could keep up the hum."

"We all thought the same thing," said Marion.

"So what does that tell us?" asked Russell. "What do we do now?"

"We do nothing," said Marion. "That's what the hum told us. We're supposed to do nothing."

"Well, there's some question in my mind as to whether that was a true message from the bear," said Bubber. "It was a little thin, if you ask me. There was nothing to grab on to."

"We all thought the same thing," said Marion.

"So what?" said Bubber. "We've been together a long time. We're starting to think alike."

"No, we were in contact with our lion," said Marion.

"I thought we were trying to contact the bear," said Bubber.

"It's the same thing," answered Marion. "When we contact the bear, we contact our lion."

"Be that as it may," Bubber went on, "We don't know that it was a message from either one of them. It was a pretty ordinary vision, if that's what it was. It didn't prove anything."

It was an argument that Marion didn't want to get into. She knew what she knew. There was no way of proving it. Or anything else for that matter, so she stayed silent. It didn't seem the time for theory.

For several days Romo kept up a pattern of humming at the mouth of the cave, driving everyone crazy in the bargain. He started at dusk and kept going until about three in the morning. Then he'd sleep most of the day and appear at the farm just before dinner time. He'd help out for a few minutes, join the group for an enormous meal, and then go back to his humming at the cave. The noise he was making was so abrasive that sleep was impossible, so they all changed over to the cat's schedule, sleeping all day and working all night. Then, just as they were starting to get used to it, Cougar made another announcement.

"I'm alright now," he said one morning. "I feel good again."

"There, you see?" said Ida, sweetly. "The hum made you feel better again."

Cougar looked at her suspiciously. "I didn't hum to feel better, I hummed for the bear to return, and where is he?"

"Maybe he wasn't supposed to return," said Bubber.

"So what's the point of humming then?" asked Cougar.

"All kinds of things happen when you hum," said Bubber, "Look what it's done for you. You've learned patience and self-mastery. Doesn't that make you feel good?"

"I could have done that a long time ago," said Cougar. "It just wasn't the right time."

CHAPTER 18

At lunch the next day Cougar told his friends at the clearing that they had too much work to handle without him, so he was canceling all his plans. He would stay there for a while and help them run things. Marion's heart leaped into her mouth when she heard the news.

"What a lovely thought," she managed to say, before catalepsy set in. "It's only right," said Cougar. "And what's right is right."

"It's a beautiful gesture," said Bubber, carefully. "Don't think for minute that it's not appreciated, but someone of your stature surely—"

"No," Cougar interrupted, "This is what's important. Maintaining all this. The ideals here. Everything—" he waved his paw around the general area.

"Don't think the thought will go unnoticed!" said Bubber, fighting hysteria, "That's what counts, remember. The thought. You don't actually have to do anything."

"No, no," said Cougar, "things have to be done. They must be done. We all have to make Sacrifices."

"Yes, but responsibilities elsewhere . . . surely must . . . weight . . . heavily . . . on your . . . " Bubber sputtered.

"First things first," said Cougar sagely. "First things first."

There was nothing more to be said or done, so Cougar stayed. And much to everyone's surprise, he actually did what he promised. He threw himself wholeheartedly into the life of the clearing, and for several days he attended to whatever job needed to be done. He weeded and cultivated, he cleaned meticulously, and he even tried his hand at cooking, which he actually did with a certain amount of flair. But after a few days his old restlessness began to set in, and after one particularly busy morning he flopped down on his side to think things over. "The truth is," he said philosophically, "I'm not cut out for this kind of work. "I think I'm really more of a planner. Maybe it would be better if I just supervised things for a while," and he got up and walked away with a serious look on his face, already preparing for the new job he'd given himself.

"Here it comes," said Marion.

"Just calm down, now," Bubber cautioned. "Let's not go looking for trouble. Everything is holding nicely."

For the next few days Cougar just mulled things over. He walked around the clearing talking to himself and measuring things with one eye closed. Then he started to examine everyone while they did their work. "Don't pay any attention to me," he said, waving them off, "just act natural. Pretend I'm not here." With all their hearts, they tried to pretend Cougar wasn't there, but with him constantly watching every move they made, they became self-conscious and awkward. Bubber dropped things, Marion burned herself, Ida slowed down so much that she started looking like a tree sloth, and Russell, to stay as inconspicuous as possible, found smaller and smaller jobs that finally became almost invisible. Cougar continued happily with his new work, taking copious notes, completely oblivious to everyone's discomfort.

When the planning stage was finished, he started in on the specifics, and the first job he tackled was the reorganization of the garden. He'd never been happy with its shape or placement, he said, and he thought it was time finally to do it right.

"What's wrong with it the way it is?" Marion asked cautiously.

"It's hard to explain," said Cougar. "You'll see when it's done."

He yelled out directions while everyone else tore down the fence and reshaped the whole thing. He watched critically while it was rebuilt to his specifications. When it was finished, he looked at it lovingly for a morning and then he proceeded to reorganize Ida. He showed her the graphs he'd made of the way she cleaned things, chiding her on her inefficiency, and demonstrated methods that would get more and better work out of her. Then since he knew everyone was bored with Marion's cooking, his next job was to replan her menus. Marion kept silent and followed his directives without so much as a hint of the tension she was feeling. But later when she was away from him she turned to Bubber for support.

"Something, eh?" she said archly.

"It's something, alright," said Bubber.

"I didn't know there was so much wrong around here," Marion said.

"Well, you live and learn," said Bubber.

It wasn't the response Marion had expected. She looked at Bubber carefully to see if his face registered some sign of irony. She couldn't find any, but she let it go. "He's just being subtle," she thought.

Evenings, Cougar decided, should be devoted to group discussions, where everyone could have the opportunity to say exactly what was on their minds. They tried it for a few nights, but there was a certain lack of spontaneity in everyone's response, and this annoyed Cougar. "What's all the moping about?" he'd say. "Nobody says anything anymore. You used to be talkative bunch."

"There's not much to say," Russell answered flatly.

"How can that be? Have you figured everything out? Did you get to the root of things before Bear left?"

"Not really," said Bubber.

"Well, then, I think we probably ought to do some more talking," Cougar said.

"Fine with me," said Russell.

"Well, let's hear something," said Cougar.

"What do you want to talk about?" Bubber asked.

"Let's talk about life," said Cougar. "Life and things of that nature."

Then, for a couple of hours, Cougar would talk about life. Once in a while, when he went completely off the mark, Bubber or Russell would gingerly try to make a point or two, but Cougar would never let them finish a sentence. He had passionate feelings about things, and if he waited too long to say them he'd lose the train of thought, so he excused himself a lot and kept interrupting. Marion refused to say anything. Ida tried a few times, but after Cougar's repeatedly telling her she didn't know what she was talking about, she just sat silently, smiling into space, and sucking on her long possum fingers. Sometimes Cougar would tell stories of experiences he'd had with the bear over the years, and sometimes he'd give demonstrations of the hum and how long he could do it without taking a breath. "I didn't know that was the idea of the hum," said Marion, cautiously. "I thought it was more where it took you, than how long you did it."

"Sophistry," said Cougar, waving Marion away. "You're an old stick-in-the-mud."

Cougar's comfort with his place at the clearing grew by the day. Then the badger twins started hanging around. They'd show up casually toward sundown, Cougar would insist that they stay, and before long they were at dinner on a regular basis. They were outgoing and talkative, but they told too many jokes, and their humor was very aggressive, and as usual, it affected Marion more than the others.

"What's going on with you, Marion?" Bubber asked her, when they found a minute away from Cougar. "Why are you so down on everything?"

"I don't like them," said Marion. "They're disruptive and they're untrustworthy."

"Give them a break, Marion," said Bubber. "They're funny and they're interesting, and it's nice to see a new face around here once in a while. Get some news of the outside world."

"They don't lift a finger to help, you'll notice. Not a dish cleaned, nothing. And I wouldn't care if they did help. They're Romo's guests, not the bear's."

"What are they doing wrong?" Bubber asked.

"Nothing. They make me uncomfortable. If I haven't learned to trust my feelings by this time, I don't belong here."

Marion vowed to be less obvious about what she felt, but it seemed to be against her nature. Her disapproval was written in every gesture, every look. She was too open, too transparent to be able to hide her feelings, and Cougar began to bristle over her coolness. Each day it bothered him more, and finally he spoke to Bubber about it.

"What's with Marion?" he asked one afternoon when they were taking a walk.

"Who?" asked Bubber, stalling for time.

"Marion," said Cougar. "What's eating her?"

"Oh, I think she just misses the bear," said Bubber. "She doesn't talk about it much, but I think she's taking it very hard.

"Well she's getting to be a pain in the neck," said Cougar. "It's hard to keep up a positive attitude with her moping around all day."

"We all have our moods," said Bubber.

"Look," said Cougar, "we have a tough situation here. It's not a time to be indulging anybody. I mean we're all suffering this thing. She's not the only one. It seems to me that we should drop our own petty problems for a minute and pull together. Don't you think?"

"I suppose so," said Bubber.

"I mean, I'm working myself sick trying to keep things organized, and I don't think she appreciates it."

He leaned into Bubber. "I feel like she has it in for me!" he said in disbelief.

"Oh, I doubt that," Bubber said.

"Yes, I really do," said Cougar. "I think she's trying to get rid of me."

"That doesn't sound like Marion," said Bubber.

"Well, that's what I feel," said Cougar. He ran around in front of Bubber and looked directly into his eyes. "I'm not asking for anything special, am I?" and there was real vulnerability in his question. It touched Bubber's heart. "No,"he said. "You're being very generous and open."

"I don't ask for any thanks, I don't need any gratitude, but a little civility wouldn't hurt, would it? Simple pleasantness? A little warmth?"

"I'll talk to her," said Bubber, eager to help patch things up between them. Later, when they were done with their chores, he took Marion for a walk.

"Romo's getting worried about you," he said when they were out of earshot of the group.

"Really?" said Marion.

"Yes," said Bubber. "He's concerned about your emotional condition."

"I think he's concerned with the fact that I see through him," said Marion. "He doesn't like the fact that I know what he's doing."

"What are you talking about, Marion?" Bubber asked.

"You don't see it?"

"I don't see anything."

"Then perhaps we shouldn't talk about it," said Marion.

"I think we'd *better* talk about it," Bubber said, and it was clear he meant it. "This think is affecting everyone and everything."

Marion bit her tongue. Talking openly about Romo was the last thing she wanted to do, but if she remained silent now the tension would grow worse, and it would prove she was the one with the problems.

"He's trying to take us over," she said breathlessly. "He's trying to run everything and discredit the bear. He wants to run the whole show. He never had the guts to face up to the bear while he was here, so now he's doing it behind his back." Marion's heart was in her mouth. "That's what he's doing," she said with finality.

"I think you're imagining things," said Bubber.

"Well, that's your opinion," said Marion.

"Romo's done nothing but help since he's been here," said Bubber.

"He's rearranged everything, and he's running everything. Nothing goes on around here without his OK. Who told him he was the boss? Who made him leader?"

"Someone's got to take that responsibility," said Bubber.

"So he volunteered," Marion said, with more than a hint of cynicism, "But who voted? Who took a vote? Who said it was alright?"

"You can't deal with change, Marion, that's your problem," said Bubber, trying to keep anger from creeping into his voice.

"You're afraid of him!" Marion said sharply. "Can't you see that? Can't you see that's what happened? Everyone's living in fear!"

"Except you," Bubber said sarcastically.

"Maybe," said Marion.

"Look," Bubber said, "Let's get down to it." He stopped walking and faced her. "According to you, the bear never does anything arbitrarily. Everything he does has a purpose. I'll accept that. I don't believe it, but for the sake of argument let's say it's true. He left us. What's the reason? At the risk of offending you, maybe the answer isn't as exalted as you might suppose. Maybe he just got sick of us. Maybe he found something more important to do with his life than hang around a bunch of misfits, pumping them up with grandiose stories and pie-in-the-sky promises to keep them from doing themselves in.

"I don't want to here this," said Marion.

"Well, you'd better face up to it," said Bubber. "Look at us. Cripples, dreamers, and misfits. Why would anyone waste his time with a bunch like us? I don't blame him for leaving. I just wish he would have said something about it first. But then again, maybe he was so embarrassed about what he'd done to us that he couldn't face us. I'm not saying that's what happened, but it's a possibility, and we'd better have the guts to face it. I don't know about you," he went on, "but I'm going to survive. What are we supposed to do, sit around for the rest of our lives humming like idiots waiting for the bear to come back? That's stupid. He's got his life to live, he's made that clear, and we have ours. You have to be prepared for anything. There are things to do. And I'm having some fun for the first time in my life."

"Fun is nothing," said Marion.

"Well, maybe you wouldn't think so if you were capable of having some."

"You spoke your piece," said Marion, calmly, "and I listened, but I won't again. You can make all the conjectures you want. I'm not interested in them. Whatever else the bear did, he's given me my life. He's given me a reason for living when I had none. He's given me a home and a purpose. He's given me companionship and support. He's shown me a picture of things that is so grand that it holds the whole world together, and nothing you can ever say is going to change that. And nothing that the bear can do is going to change it. Whatever he does, whether he comes back or not, I will love him forever." She broke from their confrontation and started waddling slowly back to the clearing, feeling old and tired. Bubber caught up with her and they walked on, each hoping the other would say something to break the tension, but it didn't happen. They returned to the clearing and busied themselves with small things to avoid the embarrassed silence. When Bubber finally left, he found himself feeling contemptuous of her and her rigidity, for her holier-than-thou attitude, and yet somewhere he knew that he was jealous. Jealous of her unbending sureness. She was absolutely devoid of any doubt about the bear's motives. It was infuriating, and unreasonable, and yet Bubber couldn't stop hoping that someday he too could feel that passionately about something. But if and when he did, he hoped it would at least be for something a little more sensible than the stubborn, mindless devotion she had for her vanished friend.

Marion's unyielding stance was costing her dearly. She had no allies to count on anymore. Bubber was off with his new friends, Russell spent his time buried beneath piles of leaves, daydreaming, and Gwen had disappeared entirely at the first sign of tension. Ida stayed nearby, but she was disoriented and turned in on herself, clinging to Marion for support. As much as Marion loved Ida, being with her took work and patience. Marion's frayed nerves were causing her to be short-tempered with Ida, and that became another irritation. She knew it was the last thing in the world Ida needed.

She also watched Bubber with growing concern as he got swept up in Cougar's life. On the surface their activities seemed harmless enough, but she saw dangerous undercurrents in everything they did together. Their singing seemed like yelling, their jokes angry, and their excursions around the mountainside, military maneuvers. Whenever she mentioned her concerns to Bubber, he would laugh her off. He was coming alive in his newfound friendship. Just the act of taking a walk with Cougar was an exciting adventure. Everyone quickly got out of their way as they came. No one wanted to tangle with them, and it filled Bubber with a great sense of power. Quite a distance to have come for a lemming, a species that cringed at even the thought of the big cats. Now he walked among them and called himself their equal. And badgers, too! An animal that despite their size could tangle with anything on four legs. And here he was, friends with them!

Sometimes the four of them would have wrestling matches, and Bubber learned all the holds, and how to fend off his opponents, or confuse them, or tie them up in knots, and it made the blood run hot through his veins. Sweating and panting, grabbing, twisting and turning, getting free of what seemed like death grips, and then, afterward, the exhaustion, the aching muscles and pounding heart; the feeling of comfort with his body. And then sitting for hours in the nearby hot springs, laughing over a particularly cunning moment of strategy or blow. Nothing had ever made Bubber so filled with himself.

Marion watched all this and said nothing, and each day her isolation grew greater. Even the solace and peace of her humming was gone from her now, since Cougar would laugh every time he heard her begin. "I can't help it," he'd say, "It's very funny. You ought to listen to yourself sometime." He'd turn away, and grab his face tightly with his paw to stifle himself, and she'd try to continue and laughter would explode out of him. It became very embarrassing for Marion, so she simply stopped the humming. To keep herself together, she began to wander off to be by herself. She'd sometimes find a pond to float in aimlessly, and then she took to writing letters to the bear. She'd scrawl them out with a stick in the dirt and then rub them out when she had finished them. This what she wrote:

"Dear Bear," she wrote, "You've been gone a long time now, and my heart is breaking. I can only stay alive by thinking that at any minute I will see your face. Will you come back, dear Bear, or is the message I feel in my heart a lie I tell myself just to survive? I think it's not a lie, but I need your voice to tell me that.

"We are not doing well without you. You are needed here in ways I don't even understand. I think the others miss you even more than I do. So much so that they pretend your absence doesn't make a difference.

"We did a hum the other night to try and find you. I am the only one who believes we did. I follow the instruction you gave us, and with all my might I try to stay silent, even though I want to do terrible things to Romo.

"I'm afraid I said too much to Bubber today. He is precariously balanced, I think, and I must be more patient with him. I hope he begins to see what Romo is doing before bad things start happening to him.

"I get angry at you sometimes, dear Bear, I confess it. I'm not as sure of things as I sound to others, and I'm confused about your leaving for so long, and not knowing where you are, but then I tell myself that there must have been a very good reason for it. Sometimes I have to say it over and over again before the hurt goes away, but it finally does. I pray that you are well. I think I would feel if you were not.

"I don't know what I will do if you don't come back.

> "Your own,
> Marion"

CHAPTER 19

Bubber was becoming more like Cougar every day—even to the depressions that started attacking him on a regular basis. Things would be going along beautifully for a while, then from out of nowhere his sense of well-being would disappear and he would be left empty and confused. He found himself this way one evening while sitting in the spring with Cougar, and his change was so immediate, so dramatic, that even the cat couldn't help noticing it.

"What's wrong?" he asked.

"I don't know," said Bubber. "These moods just come over me once in a while."

"I have them all the time," said Cougar almost proudly.

"I think I just miss the bear," said Bubber, with a touch of embarrassment. "And sometimes I think I'm angry at him for leaving. Does that sound nuts?"

"Not at all," said Cougar. "I know what you mean. It's a tough, tough situation."

"I wish he hadn't left."

"I'm pretty broken up about it myself," said Cougar.

"I wonder if he knew how much he messed everyone up," said Bubber.

"There's no way of telling what goes on in his mind," said Cougar.

"Why do you say that?" Bubber asked.

"He's a bear," said Cougar. "They have a reputation for being unpredictable."

"I didn't know that."

"Oh, yes, it's a well-known fact. They don't change

the expression on their face. He could be thinking anything, and you wouldn't know."

"Well, I miss him anyway," said Bubber.

"Yes, it's a very sad situation," said Cougar. He shook his head mournfully. Then suddenly he slapped the water with his paws. "This is stupid," he said, "We're all sitting around moping, but we haven't done the first thing to find him."

"We've done everything to find him," said Bubber.

"No, we haven't looked in the cave," said Cougar. "That's the first thing we should have done."

"I don't think so," said Bubber with some alarm.

"Yes, it should have been the first thing. It's what he would have wanted, I'm sure," said Cougar. "If he was going to leave a message, that's where it would be. It's a test. I can feel it. He's probably having a good laugh somewhere right now, waiting for us to go into the cave and find the message."

"No one's ever been in there," said Bubber uncomfortably.

"Why not?"

"Well, it's his cave. He's never invited us in there. If he'd wanted us inside, he would have said something."

"Maybe he was waiting for someone to ask."

"That doesn't sound right."

"Why not? Why wouldn't he want us in his cave?"

"I don't know. I don't want to think about it."

"'You don't want to think about it?'" Cougar repeated in disbelief. "That's quite a statement from someone who's trying to become a lion. I thought we're supposed to think about everything. I thought that's where courage lies."

"Maybe so," said Bubber, feeling pulled in two directions at once. Fears on both sides dragging him into dark and swampy places.

"I'm going in there," said Cougar. He jumped out of the spring and started walking briskly in the direction of the cave.

"I'd think twice about it," said Bubber, chasing after him. "Bear might not like it."

"He's not here. He went for a walk."

"He could come back."

Cougar stopped and turned to Bubber. "If he wasn't coming back, would you go in the cave?"

"Let's talk about something else."

"Have you ever wondered what went on in there?"

"Maybe."

"Have you ever wondered where his power comes from? His ability to know things?"

"His power comes from his lion," said Bubber. "We'll all have that power when we know ourselves as lions."

"That's what he says, but maybe it's not true," said Cougar. "What if there is no lion?" They had reached the mouth of the cave, and Cougar was peering into the darkness, his tail switching nervously back and forth. "What if he has magic in there? What if he has a rock or something that foretells things?" He was getting more and more excited, and badly unnerving Bubber. "Maybe he's got a prisoner in there," he went on. "A bat. A slave bat who goes out at night and gathers information with radar. Comes back and tells him things. That's it, I'll bet anything. He's got a bat under his power. He keeps it tame with thoughts of becoming a lion. What do you think about that?"

"I think it's nonsense."

"What if it isn't?" said Cougar, pulling nervously on his whiskers. "You can't prove it's not true, can you? You can't say for sure that it's not a possibility."

"I don't know anything!"

"Don't you owe it to yourself to see if any of this is true? You have niggling little doubts, don't you? Well, what's going to make them go away?"

"I'm going back to the clearing," said Bubber, but he made no move to go.

"Did it ever occur to you that this whole lion business was a way for him to keep himself comfy and cozy around here without doing any work? To have a lot of folks waiting on him hand and foot? No one ever challenged him—no one ever questioned him—whatever he said went—not a bad way to live, I'd say."

"I don't like this talk," said Bubber.

"Why not?" asked Cougar. "What are you afraid of?"

"I don't know," said Bubber.

"I'm not saying it's true," Cougar went on, "I'm just saying it's something to think about. If it's a possibility, it should be examined. I think I've heard the bear say that a couple of times."

"Look, this is not good stuff to think about," said Bubber. "It's making me nervous. My life has been better here at the clearing that it's ever been anywhere. Better than I ever thought possible. I don't want to trample on good things."

"What if everything you've heard about him is a myth?" said Cougar. "Wouldn't you want to know that?"

"I'm not sure," said Bubber.

"You mean you want to be living a lie?" Cougar sounded incredulous. "Mmmm. I don't like the sound of that. Not good, Bubber. I'm a little disappointed in you."

"That's the way it goes," said Bubber.

"I'm going in there," Cougar said again. "There are too many things to find out." He looked at Bubber. "Are you coming with me?"

Bubber badly needed some truth—some understanding of what was beneath things—and here seemed to be no way to go except into the unknown. "Just for one minute," he said, biting his paw, "I'll take one quick look around. I don't want to make a big production out of it."

"You'll be happy about this later on," said Cougar. "It will relieve a lot of pressure."

Tentatively they went into the cave. They waited while their eyes got used to the darkness, and when they could begin to make out shadows they started groping frantically at the walls and floor.

"Look for hidden crevices," said Cougar, trying to feel in the darkness for some secret sign.

"There's nothing in here," Bubber said quickly, desperate to leave.

"No, no, keep looking!" Cougar hissed. "He could have anticipated someone's coming in and stashed things away." He checked behind the rocks, pulling every projection, clawing at the floor, while Bubber scratched wildly at the walls, afraid of discovering something, and sorry that he had ever agreed to this. They found absolutely nothing. Not a bowl, not a morsel of food, no pine bough matting, nothing. Not a hint that anything had ever been there. The place held no secrets.

"So much for that," Bubber said quickly, with great relief. "There's nothing in here." He left the cave quickly, feeling not only that nothing had been learned, but also that a new burden had been placed on him. There was a bitter taste in his mouth, and he felt a new level of disgust and self-loathing.

"It proves nothing," said Cougar, following Bubber out of the cave. "He could have taken it with him."

"Taken *what* with him?" Bubber asked incredulously. "Some imaginary thing in your mind? He never had stuff with him. He wasn't interested in stuff. Why don't you just let it go?"

Cougar turned on Bubber with a dark look. "Are you saying I'm crazy?" he asked.

"I—" said Bubber, and shook his head. "Where did that come from?" he asked. "No one said anything about crazy. I'm just saying that there's nothing in the cave."

"What's wrong with my intuition?" asked Cougar.

"I don't follow you," said Bubber.

"Why is everyone around here allowed to have intuitions except me?"

"Everyone is allowed everything," said Bubber.

"I've just shared very private feelings with you," said Cougar, "and I don't want to be treated like a fool for it. Do you understand?"

"Yes, I do," said Bubber. "If I gave you that impression, it wasn't intentional."

Cougar pointed a warning claw at Bubber. "Openness is not easy for me. When I attempt it, I will not be mocked. Is that clear?"

"Yes, it is," said Bubber. "I'm sorry."

"I won't say it again," said Cougar, and it was clear from his tone that he wouldn't. Something other than speech would happen the next time, and Bubber was loath to think what that might be. He racked his brain for what he had done that could have upset the cat so terribly, but he came up with nothing, which only added to his feelings of confusion and despair.

When Bubber got back to the clearing, Marion was seething. She was cleaning everything in sight in order to keep from flying into a rage. She was breathing hard, her movements were stiff and jerky, and she wouldn't look at Bubber.

"Now what?" Bubber said curtly. "What's the problem?"

"You know the problem," said Marion, almost inaudibly.

"What's on your mind?" said Bubber. "If you say what's on your mind, maybe you'd stop feeling so miserable for a minute."

Marion dropped what she was doing and whirled on Bubber. "What were you doing in the bear's cave?" she blurted, fire in her eyes. "Who gave you permission to go in there?"

"Who says I was in the cave?" said Bubber.

"Do you deny it?"

"Since when do I have to report to you, Marion? Do you want me to start writing little notes about my day's activities and then check with you to see if they're alright? Is that what you want, Marion?"

"Were you in the bear's cave?"

"I don't have to account to you!"

"What are you afraid of, Bubber? Either you were in his cave, or you weren't."

"I don't want you following me around," said Bubber.

"I wasn't following you around," said Marion. "Ida walked past the cave and heard voices. The cave amplifies sound, and the voices were yours and Romo's. Ida came back and told me. Do you have any objection?"

"Yes, I do. I want you to mind your own business, and that goes for Ida too."

"The bear's business is my business," said Marion.

"I can say that too, Marion."

"Yes, but you're not *living* it. No one gave you the right to examine his quarters, to spy on him, to ransack his home. He wouldn't do that to *your* things." There was authority in her tone, an evenness, that was formidable, and Bubber found himself afraid of her.

"You're being a little dramatic, Marion," he said. "We were simply looking for clues to his whereabouts."

"You're lying, Bubber."

"You're not my conscience," Bubber yelled. "Get out of my head and mind your own business!"

"I'm not sure I'm going to do that," said Marion evenly. The time for silence was over. The bear and his work were being undermined, and the erosion was no longer slow. Something had to be done, and she felt she was the only one left to do it. As the argument with Bubber continued, she found herself reaching out to her lost friend. "Bear!" she called, silently in her own head. "Bear! Hear Me! Answer me! Am I doing what you want? Am I doing your work the way you would do it?" The bear she pictured in her mind remained still and calm. He gave no answer, but nothing compelled her to stop the tack she was taking.

"You've been argumentative and grouchy since the bear left," said Bubber. "No one's been able to communicate with you at all. Things are hard enough around here without your moods."

"I have been upset since the bear left, that's true, but I have been *fearful* since Romo got here. Those are two different things." Ida, Russell, and Gwen, hearing the noise, left their jobs and came to the clearing to see what was wrong. They listened carefully but made no attempt to join in. "He's tearing us apart!" Marion cried, pleading with her wings, "Don't you see it? He's set himself up as the voice of the bear, but he's not! He's never loved him! He never followed the bear's teaching when the bear was with us. Now that the bear is gone we're all supposed to run after Romo and worship him. He's trying to rip us away from the bear! He's trying tot make us suspect everything the bear taught us. But there's no love in Romo, no peace, no gentleness. We're all afraid of him! Can't you see that? And if we're afraid of him, what can he possibly teach us?" She looked to her friends for some sign of support; a nod, a phrase, anything, but none was forthcoming. "That's what's going on here," she continued, "and that's why I'm depressed, and that's why I'm afraid." She sank to the ground. There was nothing more to say, no way to reach into them. Her friends were paralyzed with embarrassment and confusion. Their fears had a taken a tight hold on them, and they clung to them as allies, and remained silent.

"Why don't you leave?" Romo said quietly.

Marion whirled around at the sound of his voice. He was sitting motionless in the dark, just at the rim of the clearing. Her heart leaped into her mouth.

"I don't want to," she said quickly.

"You're not happy here. Why don't you go someplace where you'll find peace?" said Romo, his eyes gleaming in the darkness. "There's nothing here for you any more," he went on, "You're depressed and gloomy, and your misery infects everything around you. The rest of us are trying to make a life together, and you fill us with morbidity. There's no joy in you. You live in the past. In false hopes. You can't face reality or deal with anyone around you. You have no feeling for the rest of the group, and now you're trying to sow unrest and suspicion amongst us. It's not good, Marion. Why don't you leave?"

"I don't take instruction from you, Romo," said Marion, quietly, trying to maintain as much equilibrium as she could muster. She knew that if she lost control it would be the end of everything. Her friends sat like ghosts, not helping, not participating, each hoping that something would happen all by itself to make everything good again. She knew that somewhere, deep within themselves they were still her allies. Somewhere they loved her. But she couldn't find that place in them now. Their fears were right out in front of them now, and they had the face of a cat.

"We are here at the clearing at the bear's invitation," said Marion. She braced herself and swallowed hard. "I'll leave when he tells me to. Not before."

"There's no bear here," said Romo. "Your bear has abandoned you. We have the choice of maintaining an ordered and happy community without him, or to re-treat into chaos and fairytales. If you can't stand the truth, then leave. We won't spend the rest of our lives living in a fantasy world. We are alive *now. Here. This moment. In this place.* If you won't contribute to that, then leave."

Marion turned to her friends. "Do you believe what he said? Do you believe that I've been underhanded and cunning?"

"I don't know if you've been all that," Bubber said tentatively. "But I do know that you've been very depressing to be around these days. You make everyone feel guilty, and I don't know what that serves. I think whatever happened to you before you came to the clearing makes it impossible for you to accept the fact that the bear walked out on us. But he did. Let's fact it. He walked out on us. He's gone. Maybe he's lost, maybe he's dead, maybe he just got sick of us, who knows? Maybe he just got into one of his fogs and forgot who he is. To tell you the truth, if he is alright,

- 154 -

and he does come back, I'll have a lot of questions to ask him before I feel comfortable with him again. And you know Bear, maybe he'll answer them, maybe he won't, depending on his mood. If he does answer them, I don't know if I'll believe him, and if he doesn't, I'll be unsettled and confused forever. But the bear does what he wants, doesn't he? It's his party. It's always been his party. That's all I have to say."

"Yes, but now it's Romo's party," said Marion. "Do you prefer that?"

"I don't know what I prefer, Marion," said Bubber. "My brain hurts. I don't want you to leave, but I can't stand any more philosophy, and I can't stand any more guilt. I just want to live my small life in peace and quiet for a minute. Who am I anyway? I'm nothing. Why should I be worried about solving the problems of the universe? It's stupid. I'm sick of it. For once in my small life I want to have a little fun without feeling guilty. What's wrong with that? That's not a whole lot to ask."

"That's pretty much the way I feel," said Russell.

"Do you want me to go?" Marion asked, and there was so little emotion in her voice that it made the question even more terrible. Russell cleared his throat and started to say something, but by the cautious way he was beginning Marion could see that it was going to be conciliatory, and it was too late for that. She put up a wing, silencing him. "Don't say anything," she said, and she started to walk off.

"I'd like to speak," said Russell.

"I don't want to hear it, whatever it is," said Marion. "My one comfort is that I don't think any of you know what you're doing." She turned to Cougar. "Except you, Romo. You know exactly what you're doing." At another time, her fiery look would have enraged the cat, but he smiled condescendingly and let it pass. Marion surveyed the clearing to see if there was something she wanted to take with her, some last thing to say to this group that had been her life for so many years, but nothing came to mind. She sighed and gathered herself up to leave, wondering whether to even bother saying goodbye, when a huge crow glided slowly down from a nearby fir and sat watching them from one of the rocks. Cougar looked up in annoyance. It wasn't a time that he wanted company. He coughed loudly in his fist. The crow glanced over at him, and Cougar shot him a terrifying look, hoping it would send him on his way, but the bird just nodded back. "Hi, there," he said amiably.

"Pardon me," said Cougar as politely as he could. "This is a private discussion. If you have business here, come back in a couple of hours."

"Don't mind me," said the crow, "I'm just taking it easy here for a minute. Go ahead with whatever you're doing. I'll be gone before you know it."

It wasn't the response Cougar had expected. He shook his head and tried again. "I guess you didn't hear me. This isn't a public meeting. We have private things to discuss. Take off."

"I heard you fine," said the bird. "Like I said, I'm just resting here. I'll be gone as soon as I catch my breath." He began preening himself, smoothing his feathers and pulling pieces of things from between his toes. A warning sign flashed through Cougar's head, but he disregarded it. "Impossible," he thought. "The bird's just an idiot."

"I'll say it one last time," he began, but the bird interrupted him.

"Excuse me," he said, "but isn't this the clearing where there's a bear who kind of presides over things?"

"Sort of," said Cougar.

"Oh, good," said the bird, laughing with relief. "Thanks. I got confused for a minute. I thought I was in the wrong place."

Cougar stared in disbelief. "Listen," he said, "did I just say something to you, or am I going crazy?"

"No, you're not going crazy," said the crow, "I heard

you very well. You told me to leave. But I'm a crow, and I have safe passage here. All crows do. Ask the bear if you don't believe me."

"He's not here."

"Well, ask him when he comes back," said the crow definitively. He pulled a particularly long piece of straw from under his wing and dropped it generally in Cougar's direction.

"I don't take orders from crows," Cougar said.

"No, of course not," said the bird. "I forgot myself for a minute. Let me rephrase that. "If you would *kindly* ask the bear when he returns, you'd find that my presence might not fill him with displeasure."

"He's not coming back," said Cougar warily.

"Oh, that's hard to believe," said the crow dramatically. "Why not?"

"I really don't want to talk about it," said Cougar. He looked up and noticed that there were now several more crows in the trees above him. It was not a pleasant sight. Something. Something was afoot, and until he got a sense of what they were up to, he decided to stall a little.

"Forgive me for being nosey," said the crow, "But you know what we're like. Into everything. We just can't seem to let anything go. It drives everyone a little crazy, but that's the way it is." He leaned toward Cougar and in a loud whisper said, "So what's the dirt on the bear? Did he pass away or what?"

"We don't know," said Cougar. "He just left."

"He just *left*? Just like *that*?" asked the crow in abject disbelief.

"That's right," said Cougar,

"He turned things over to you?"

"I've taken on some of his responsibilities in his absence."

"Out of the kindness of your heart."

"Something like that."

"You must be quite something. Did the bear ask you to do that?"

"Not in so many words."

"Not in so many words. Did these folks take a vote on it?"

"It wasn't necessary."

"Sounds like a takeover to me."

It was a very brash statement and Cougar examined the crow carefully for a trace of humor or at least irony, but he saw none.

"You're wrong," he said. "Ask them if you don't believe me." He nodded in the direction of his friends.

The crow surveyed the motley group and shot them a disapproving look. "Are they capable of speech? Can they think? Walk around? Things like that?"

Whatever his game was, the bird was going too far. It was time to put a stop to the foolishness. "I've had enough questions now," Cougar said, staring down the bird.

"Let's forget the formalities," said the crow, cutting through Cougar's threat. "We know all about you. We know what you're doing. You're a bully and a coward. You never had the guts to look the bear in the eye while he was here, and now that he's gone you think you can fill his place. Well, let me give you a little free advice. It will be a cold day in China."

"I'm warning you," Cougar growled. "be careful of what you say."

"I'm not finished," said the crow defiantly. "You've never followed one instruction in your life without making a hash out of it, you've never changed one single thing about yourself, and you mock each effort that these poor boobs make to better their own miserable selves. Some leader. You can't keep *yourself* together, let alone these misfits, and when this experiment disintegrates because of your cunning and divisiveness, you'll wander off thinking that you're special because you've been able to ruin everything the bear built. I should let it happen too. I have no real right to interfere. The bear won't care, and this bunch of cowards doesn't deserve much better, but I don't like what you're doing to the duck. She's suffered enough."

"Crow," said Cougar, "take a look at me. Take a look at what stands before you, and ask yourself if what you are doing is wise." His voice was a thin rasp, and there was a glint in his eye that had not been seen before at the clearing. But in his mounting anger he neglected to notice the number of crows that were now crowding the trees all around him. *"Cat,"* the crow countered, "We have approached you before, and it's *you* who are warned! Don't make me remind you of—"

In mid-sentence Cougar leaped and struck. The blow was so fast that no one saw it. A handful of black feathers floated to the ground, and the crow was silenced forever. With great effort Cougar tried to pull himself back into a semblance of control. It was instantly clear to him that his position was now very precarious. "I hope you can understand what's just transpired," he said uneasily. There was no response from his stunned audience. Violence had left their life at the clearing long ago, and Cougar's awful act immediately put everything into perspective. The spell that they had been living under was broken. "There's some sort of conspiracy going on here," Cougar shouted fearfully, "and we all know who's perpetrating it! We're going to have unity here, and if there's a price, then it will have to be paid!" It wasn't going over. He began to scream at the awestruck group, berating them, as if they were responsible for what had just happened, as if they had forced him into his terrible act.

Then the crows struck. A storm of them fell on the clearing, adding to those who were already there, and they blotted out the moon and the stars. A cyclone of them swirled around the cat, engulfing him with their bodies. Then, as quickly as the crows had come, they flapped away. Cougar careened around the clearing, shrieking madly, grabbing at his face with one paw, and batting at the vanished birds with another. "Help me!" he screamed. "Help me! Get them away from my eyes!" He ran in jagged circles, falling all over himself, writhing and twisting on the ground, bashing into trees, and burning himself in the fire, while everyone watched frozen in horror. Eventually he found a path away from the clearing and went shrieking off into the woods. His anguished cries could be heard all that night, and throughout most of the next day.

Cougar was not seen in that part of the world again. From time to time word of his progress would drift back to those at the clearing, and according to the stories they heard his wounds healed quickly. He survived the shame, and the helplessness, and slowly, slowly over the years he came to accept his blindness. Sometime later he even learned to feel a little gratitude toward those few friends who kindly brought him food to eat and led him around from place to place. And eventually, after many years, so the stories went, he even began to learn some lessons in patience and humility.

CHAPTER 20

For many days it was very quiet at the clearing. Work was done slowly and carefully, and Bubber, Russell, and Ida each deeply probed into their own complicity in the events that had taken place. Marion once again became the mother to all her friends, and her warmth without any hint of recrimination helped to slowly heal the pain they all were feeling. Bubber tried desperately to come to some resting place in his mind— some solid understanding of what things now meant to him, what universe he inhabited. But all he could arrive at with any certainty was a deep sense of guilt at the way he had treated Marion, and he knew that before any other pieces fit together that the first thing he had to do was apologize to her. But the sense of his own failure was so overwhelming that it took many days to have the courage to even approach her, and when finally he did find the courage she was never alone. When she was alone she was too busy. Finally the weight became so heavy that he just went up to her at a completely inappropriate time. "Marion," he blurted, in a loud and awkward voice, "Please forgive me!" He fell at her feet and sobbed as if his whole body would break apart. Before long she too was crying and stroking him with her wing, much as she had done on the first night she had met him. "Everything changes and nothing changes," she thought.

Once Bubber had broken the ice with his apology, each of the others, in their own time and their own way begged forgiveness from Marion, and for each it was as painful, and as cathartic. Though Marion had never blamed them for anything, she was happy that the dreadful tensions were breaking apart, that they were learning important things about themselves. Speech came back to the clearing. They savored their companionship in a new way. The talk now was quieter. More contemplative. Less concerned with ultimate meanings and more with moment-to-moment peace and order.

Once the shock of the previous weeks had passed, Bubber tried tentatively to re-examine his feelings about the bear, but nothing came to him except a hollowness and a wound. He was careful not to allow it to turn into a sense of betrayal, he knew now that those feelings would lead him into dangerous territory. But he was confused and in pain about the loss of his teacher and friend and guide. He couldn't stop feeling that way, and there was no way to deny it. When prodded gently, Russell had to admit that he felt the same way.

The closeness that he and Bubber shared started to grow deeper, though now it tended to express itself in less dramatic ways—in small and thoughtful kindnesses rather than long, passionate discussions. Then one day Russell went back to the kind of movement that was given to his species. At first it seemed to Bubber that this was a defeat, and it disturbed him. But Russell soon convinced him that it was the right thing to do.

"It was a useless exercise, the rolling," he confessed. "I have to face it. This was the body I was given. Why pretend otherwise? Rolling around like a mouse in heat won't get me any closer to perfection, or my lion, or whatever it is one gets close to."

"What about all that?" Bubber asked cautiously, sensing a doubt or two in his friend about where he was ultimately headed.

"What about all what?" said Russell.

"The lion business," said Bubber.

Russell thought carefully before answering. "I don't know what to think about it," he said finally. "I have more pressing things to worry about at the moment."

"My sentiments exactly," said Bubber.

"I know one thing," said Russell, "I miss the bear terribly. It's an ache that stays with me all the time, and it won't go away."

"I feel that way too," said Bubber.

"The trick is not to blame him for the ache."

"Yes, that's the trick," Bubber agreed.

Russell started spending most of his days in silent contemplation. He'd lie for hours at a time at the edge of the clearing staring off into space. He did his work, and was warm and friendly, but whenever there was nothing specific to do, he'd go back to his position on the rim of the clearing and focus on the horizon. Sometimes Bubber would join him for a few minutes. He'd stretch himself out alongside of Russell and share the silence with his friend, and often he'd feel that in these silences more was exchanged than in their old heated discussions. Friendship and love didn't seem to need a lot of words, he began to discover. Nor even a lot of activity.

One afternoon after a particularly long silence Russell spoke. "He's out that way, Bubber. He's past the mountains in that direction."

"Bear?"

Russell nodded.

"How do you know?"

"I don't know how I know."

"Did you hear his voice in your ear? Did you have a vision?"

"No, I just know where he is," Russell said, seeming to listen to some distant voice, "and he's alright too."

"Well, that's very good to hear," said Bubber.

"You don't believe me, do you?" Russell asked with a smile.

Bubber thought a long time before answering. "Russell, I think I've stopped believing in just about everything. I know that sounds very negative, but I don't mean it that way. I just can't concern myself with a lot of believing right now. Maybe some day I'll get back to it, but when I do, I hope it will be with more conviction than I've been able to muster up in the past. I want to trust myself a little better before I start believing in a lot of things again. Do you know what I mean?"

"I do," said Russell. "I feel the same way, mostly. But I do believe the bear is out that way." He pointed his head toward the distant mountains.

"What makes you so sure?"

"I don't know," said Russell, "but he is, and I have to go out and find him."

Bubber looked out at the panorama stretched out before him. "You say he's past those mountains?" he asked anxiously.

"I believe so, yes."

"Russell, those mountains are weeks away from here. I can't even guess at how far they are. And they're covered with deep snow, too. You can't move in that stuff, you don't have the right equipment. And you wouldn't survive that kind of cold either. It sounds like a bad idea to me."

"Well, I've got to find him," Russell said softly.

"Russell, I'd think about it for a while before I did something like this."

"I need to see him."

"Yes, we all do," said Bubber. "We all need to see him. We've been through that. But I promise you, Russell, this isn't wise. I really suggest you talk to someone who's been that route. See what you're in for. That's rugged country out there, and you're terrible physical condition."

"Not so bad, actually, since I stopped the rolling."

"No, you're in bad shape, Russell, face up to it."

"It's probably not a rational move," Russell

conceded, "but I've thought about it a lot. I know he's out there, and I have to go and look for him."

"Well, I think you're right when you say it's not rational. It sounds very self-destructive, Russell. Have you examined it carefully? It sounds like it's coming from some kind of despair. It's like the rolling. It's another way to beat yourself up. What do you need that for? You're past all that."

"No, it isn't any of that," Russell said very gently, "I just need to be with the bear."

There was no passion in Russell's tone. He had obviously come to this decision slowly and thoughtfully, and was simply preparing himself for the exact moment that he would leave. Each activity of his now became a step in this preparation. There was no exercise, no attempts to learn survival int he snow; it was the set of his mind. The quiet and single-minded way he approached things. The complete attention he gave to everyone. Even Ida was treated with gentleness and respect. He really listened to her now, patiently trying to find the thread in everything she said, and as a result, almost magically, she began to make more sense. With someone paying attention to her, she started to communicate more clearly.

Bubber watched Russell's preparations with a mixture of fear and wonder. It was watching someone prepare to die, and Bubber was sure that the whole exercise was the sign that Russell had simply given up. That he just wanted to end it all. He wanted to talk about it with his friend, but he knew it was futile.

Then one morning, right after breakfast, Russell announced quietly that it was time for him to go. He sat with his friends for a few moments soaking up impressions of the place that was the only real home he'd ever know, engraving them on his memory, and then he started slowly off. His friends followed him to the edge of the clearing, and then they gave him a long embrace, gathering up as much of him as they could. They put him down gently and Russell slithered off, stopping once to look back and smile at his friends before disappearing into the saplings and shrubs. They watched the grasses sway this way and that as he made his way down the mountainside, and when they lost sight of his movement they followed the route he would take for the next weeks. Their eyes moved upward through the long fertile valley beneath them, then further to the rougher foothills on the rise up again, and then into the forbidding ice castles that seemed to dare anyone to even come near. Then silently they went back to work, staying very close to each other to keep the loneliness from crowding in.

The next morning, just after sunrise, Gwen came prancing into the clearing. She had been gone for days, and no one had even noticed. There was a look of expectancy in her eyes, and she pawed the ground nervously for a moment before she spoke.

"I'm going home," she said tentatively. "I'm going back to my people, and I wanted to say goodbye before I left." She paused, waiting for some response, but none came. "More than anything I'd like to stay here with you, but I can't. Again she waited for a reaction. "If this isn't interesting to you, I can certainly understand why. I have been pretty depressing to be with, I suppose, but it was my own self-hatred, nothing any of you have done. I want you to know that. I have a family, you see. I have a mate and children, and I've abandoned them all this time, and it weighs on me. I wasn't good at family life. I failed in every aspect of it, and I left thinking that they would be better off without me, but I know now that I did the wrong thing. Even if what I felt was true, it was the wrong thing. I have to go back and face whatever damage I've done. I want you to know that my time at the clearing has been the only happiness I've ever know. You've saved my life, and more than anything I want to be able to come back someday. I pray for that with all my heart, but I must also recognize that it might not be possible. So," she said quietly, "Since I might not be seeing you again, I just wanted to thank you for your kindness and patience."

She waited for a sign from the group that they understood, that they cared for her even a little, that they had even heard her, but they looked back at her with blank eyes. It was too much for them, and the wrong time, and they couldn't speak.

"Well, that's all I wanted to say," Gwen whispered, "I hope I haven't caused you any problems." She pawed at the ground for a moment, still hoping for some sort of response. None came. She turned quickly and left.

"A fine time she picked," Marion said bitterly. "She's never shared herself for a minute with anyone. She sopped up everything we had and never gave a thing back. Good riddance, I say. It will be a breath of fresh air without her." She turned back to her cleaning and buried herself in her work.

Bubber tried to join her. He picked up a pine scrub and began scouring their food bowls, but a restlessness gnawed at him. He fought knowing what it was, but it overtook him. With a curse, he threw the pine scrub violently across the clearing and headed out into the woods.

"Where are you going!" Marion demanded. There had been enough comings and goings, and she wasn't about to let anyone out of her sight anymore.

"I'm going to find Gwen."

"What for?"

"To say goodbye. To wish her well."

"She doesn't need your blessings."

"Well, maybe she does."

"She's looking for forgiveness, but she hasn't done anything to earn it."

"Her work is with her family. She's got to do it there first. She knows that. If we don't give her our blessings, she'll muck up what she went back to fix."

"She's learned nothing from being here!"

"That's not for you to say," Bubber answered, and he ran out of the clearing.

Marion's whole body went into a spasm of anger and frustration. She shrieked out in pain, but the words that flew from her were, *"Then give her my blessings too!"* Her voice was clenched and tormented, and she wanted not to have said this, but she could not stop herself. With all the pain and confusion she felt, her goodness, and the purity of her heart would not be stopped. It insisted on coming through.

CHAPTER 21

Bubber ran on, muttering and cursing under his breath at the problems Gwen had created, and at his own mounting sense of responsibility that hung on him like a dead weight. He knew that what she was doing was the right thing. There would be no peace for her anywhere till she came to terms with what she had abandoned. Not only was it the right thing for her to do, it was the only possible right. Often there were choices, different paths to take, but in Gwen's case this was the only road. The only way she could continue with herself. He didn't want to know so much about her, or to care so much either. But somehow he felt that if she succeeded with her task it would make his own road a little easier to travel. He also knew that if he let her go with bitterness in his heart he would be tied to her forever. It was a burden he didn't want to live with. If something happened to her on her way home or if she failed in her dealing with her family he'd hate himself for the rest of his life, and it would be even worse for poor Marion, who always managed to take things harder than anyone. Still, it wasn't a time that he wanted to be gallivanting all over the countryside looking for her. Who knew what direction she was headed anyway, or how far she had gotten? He scurried through the underbrush, taking a shortcut to the river that wound its way down the mountainside. Before long he heard a clamoring that mixed with the roar of water as it fell over the falls and into the gorge, and as he got nearer the sounds broke into barks and grows. He rounded a bend in the river wall and saw Gwen, her eyes on fire, and foaming at the mouth, holding off a pack of starving wild dogs. They had her cornered at a curve in the river where the gorge fell in a sheer drop of a hundred feet. Bubber watched in terror as the dogs closed on her, nipping at her heels, trying to get her to turn her back long enough so that a hold could be caught on her neck. But she refused to remain still. She kicked and turned and bucked, moving so fast that they couldn't grab her anywhere. There was desperation in their eyes as they tried their maneuvers on her, but they also knew that her energy could not last forever. That if they managed to keep her cornered, she would finally tire and then one of them would make one lunge and catch hold hard enough to throw her off balance. It was a just a matter of time. One of the dogs snapped and caught her on the ankle, but she flung him off. Another leapt at her rear, another clawed at her flanks, but Gwen bucked back and forth, threw him up in the air and then kicked him hard in the throat before he landed. Blood ran down her ankle, and another trickle appeared at her chest. Her breath came in rasps, and she began to sense the end of her resistance. The dogs felt it too. There was a pause in the fighting. A frozen moment that almost seemed homage to the deer, then the dogs slowly repositioned themselves for the kill. As they prepared to spring, Gwen suddenly threw herself up on her hind legs, twisted around completely and threw herself into the chasm. Without a hesitation the dogs retreated into the woods looking for other prey. Bubber ran frantically to the edge of the precipice and looked to see where she had fallen. Miraculously, she'd landed in the center of the river, but had grazed her head on a boulder that lay just beneath the surface of the water. She floated unconscious with her head bobbing in and out of the water, held back from the force of the current by the rock that she had struck. Without thinking Bubber leaped off the edge of the cliff, and landed upstream of Gwen. Struggling with the current he veered over to where she lay, and braced himself to the best of his ability on the rock beneath her, and pushed with all his might to keep her head out of the water. He shouted to her at the top of his lungs, trying to wake her up, choking on the water that filled his lungs and trying to deal with her tremendous weight at the same time. "Wake up! Wake up, Gwen!" he shouted through the roar of the falls, and she did for a brief moment, but she passed out again, and her body was like a piece of driftwood, bobbing up and down in the current. Bubber strained and pushed, but her size and weight was too much for him, and he began to slip off the corner of the rock that he'd hooked himself on. Sputtering and coughing, breathing in as much water as air, he gave one mighty shove, using the last of his strength, and at that moment Gwen came loose from the rock. Her body swung around, pushing Bubber along with her, and she sped with the current downstream, and then drifted to the far bank, where she came to rest with Bubber trapped beneath her in the shallow water. Before long she began to breathe, and then, coughing and sputtering, she woke with a start, and scrambled to her feet, only to see Bubber floating near her at the shore, lifeless and limp, just under the surface of the water. She grabbed his body up in her teeth, pulled it out of the water, and dragged it onto a pile of leaves on the bank. She nipped and pawed at his limp body to no avail, and then began shrieking for help. Over and over again she shouted, weeping and digging into him, nudging him with her head, in an attempt to bring him around. "Help!" she shrieked, "Help, somebody please!" But a crow had already seen everything, and sped to the clearing to tell Marion and Ida. Breathlessly they raced to the river and joined Gwen in an attempt to pull Bubber around, but they were too late.

"He saved my life," Gwen wailed through her shock

and exhaustion. "I maligned him, I ignored him, and he killed himself for me." She fell to the ground and began sobbing. It was more than Ida and Marion could deal with. They had seen too much loss, and their suffering would have to be meted out in small increments now for them to want to go on at all. They watched numbly while Gwen spent her emotions, then the three of them began dragging their friend's body back to the clearing where it could be buried underneath the sheltering trees he loved so much.

When Bubber came through the corridor, he was blinded by the light of a thousand suns. It came in great pulsating waves, surrounding him and sweeping through him. It was new and surprising and the most familiar thing that he had ever known. A lion was there with him, massive and regal and the lion was created by the light, and the lion was the light, and the lion was the bear.

"You're a little premature," said the lion, beaming at Bubber, "but we are delighted to see you. Your courage is noted, and is much appreciated."

"Well, you do what you have to do," said Bubber, with more than a little pride. "To be honest, I didn't anticipate the consequences."

"And that is part of what is esteemed," said the lion who was the bear. "You have done very well."

"I'm happy you feel that way," said Bubber, beaming back at the lion-bear with a great radiance of his own. He looked down at himself in surprise and saw flaming paws, and shimmering around him he felt a golden sun of a mane, and flying behind him was a blazing comet of a tail.

"Do you know yourself?" asked the bear who was a lion. "I think I do," Bubber answered.

"And what are you?" asked the lion who was a bear.

"I seem to be a lion," said Bubber.

"You are that," said the lion who was a bear. "You are that, my son. You are that which you have feared. You are that which you have denied, and you are that from which you have run. You are that which has no end and no beginning. You are that which is great, you are that which is wise, you are that which is good. You are that which is everywhere and you are that which is forever. You are the lion." And the lion who was the bear smiled at him in his completeness, and joy filled both of them, and they knew who they were, and they both became the light, and they were one. And the bear who was a lion showed him all things, and they went to all places that have ever been. They found the beginning of things and the ends of things. They traveled through infinite space and discovered worlds without end. They saw life being formed, and galaxies swirl together, they watched universes explode and disintegrate and be reborn again. They saw beauty beyond words and knew joy beyond description. And after they saw all things and went all places the lion who was a lemming felt himself pulling back into his old shape. His old lemming shape, which fixed him in time and place, and was small and heavy and insignificant. He tried to will it away. To shrug it off him and stay as the light, but the lemming wouldn't leave him alone.

"What is it?" he asked, "What's happening to me?"

"As far as you have come, and your distance has been considerable, it seems your lemming needs you still."

"I am a lion," said Bubber. "I know myself as a lion now. I have no interest in lemmings."

"But his presence tells us otherwise," said the bear, as gently as he could.

- 173 -

"I threw my life away for another animal," said Bubber plaintively, "an animal I didn't even like very much. Isn't that enough? Lemmings don't do things like that."

"A significant act, without question," said the bear, "but here you are again in the fur."

"But I like it here," Bubber protested. "I feel real now. I have a handle on something tangible. I know things. I don't want to go back to all that confusion."

"Don't be afraid," said the lion who was a bear, "Your progress is real. You have come a true distance. I think you'll be pleasantly surprised."

CHAPTER 22

Gwen, Ida, and Marion dragged Bubber's body back to the clearing and dug him a grave beneath the tree that had become his own. They placed him in the hole and stared down at the remains of their friend, not knowing what to do. A soft wind blew through the trees, adding to their desolation.

"Should something be said?" Gwen whispered. "Should something be spoken? Some last thoughts of some kind?"

"Say them," Marion murmured, knowing she couldn't have gotten out a word.

"I'm not good at these things," said Gwen, her old fears coming right back into place. No one spoke.

"Marion, I wasn't close to him," Gwen insisted. "I didn't know him." Still no one spoke.

She started to say something and froze. "I could say the wrong thing," she thought, "Alienate them even further." It was a paltry thought next to what Bubber had done, and the selfishness of it sickened her. "Face the fear, for God's sake!" She ordered herself, "Face the embarrassment! He killed himself for you!" She took a deep breath and plunged into her heart.

"We send our thoughts with this young lion," she said almost inaudibly, "That they may accompany him on his journey to his true home. We wrap him in wings of love, with the sure knowledge that he is going to that place where there is no pain, no fear, and no death. Where he will be forever with the bear in peace, in joy and perpetual understanding. We send him our eternal gratitude for this great sacrifice that has been made on our behalf. May we never forget what he has done, and may we learn to give ourselves for the sake of others, as he has given of himself for us. Goodbye, dear friend."

As Marion listened, it became impossible for her not to feel the love and compassion pouring out of Gwen. "Thank you," she said when Gwen had finished, "that was very beautiful." It was all she could get out, but Gwen heard in the words the forgiveness that she had hoped for. Hesitantly they began to throw dirt in the grave, and with the first handful Bubber coughed up the entire river. Great geysers of water and dirt flew out of his mouth, covering everyone with mud. "Oh, my God," said Marion, "He's alive. Get him out of there. Get him out!" They pulled Bubber out of his grave and pressed on him and pummeled him until in self-defense he started to fight them off. He had enough problems without being beaten up by his friends. "What are you doing?" he called out in alarm. "Get off of me!"

"You saved my life," said Gwen, alternately weeping and laughing hysterically. "I've maligned you, I've berated you, I've spurned you, and you did this for me, oh God, oh God!" she cried, wailing with the pent-up emotions of years. "That's enough now," said Bubber, beating her off. "Get back to your children. Go tend to your family before it's too late." He got up gingerly and looked around to try and get his bearings, but it was hopeless, so he lay down and slept for a day and a half.

When Bubber finally awoke he felt as if his brain had been replaced by a hot potato. He wandered around the clearing holding his head, unable to keep his balance, and grabbing at things to keep from falling down. It was as if his whole center of gravity had shifted inside of him to a new and undefinable place. Ida told him it was just a headache or so, but he wasn't convinced. He sat down beneath his tree and tried to organize his mind and see if he could get it to slow down, and then he remembered what had just happened to him. Where he had been. At first he thought it was a dream, but snatches of conversation and feelings were so vivid and rich in his memory that he soon knew it was real.

"I've just been with the bear," he told Marion, who had been watching his behavior warily.

"That's nice," said Marion.

"No, I mean, really," said Bubber. "I've really been with the bear. He appeared to me as the lion, and he was blazing with light, and we explored the universe together. I knew myself as a lion. It's all true, Marion. Everything he told us is true."

"I know that," said Marion. She seemed happy that Bubber now had a dream that they could share. The dream that she had been having for so long. Her reaction made Bubber pause. Perhaps it was a dream. Perhaps his brush with death had caused hallucinations. He tried to let his images go, but they stayed with him and as he became stronger they got even more intense. Then as the burning in his head subsided and his balance returned he found that a new change was taking place in him. Light of varying intensity began appearing around everything. He'd shake his head to rid himself of these ghost images, but they wouldn't go away, and soon he had no alternative but to accept them. And when he did so, he could see that the light played differently around everything he looked at. Every tree was surrounded by its own multicolored halo. Each animal. Every stone on the ground shone with its own radiance. The tumbled boulders that gave the clearing its distinction glowed with a special, blazing intensity. And on each of his friends, his beloved Ida and Marion, he could see outlined the shapes of the lions that they were fast becoming. "I can see it,

Marion!!" he shouted gleefully the first time it appeared. "I can see your lion! It's fully formed and surrounds you in a brilliant golden light!" Marion smiled shyly, caught between fear for his mind and a desperate need to share in the fantasy. She chose to compliment him on his vision and go about her business.

Bubber tried to keep his excitement from spilling out all over, from confusing everyone, but too much was happening and he couldn't hold it to himself. "I don't know what's happened to me, Marion, but I know that everything the bear said to us was true. I can see it. I can feel it. Our lions are with us all the time. The bear is here with us. He's at the clearing most of the time. Watching us. Protecting us in ways you can't see yet. Keeping certain things away. Bringing other things in. He's never left us, Marion, that's why he didn't tell us he was going away. He's here right now. This minute. I can see him. He can see me."

Marion and Ida listened to him carefully. They believed not one word he was saying, but his passion and his vision were comforting to them, so they let him continue his ranting and raving. He even began drifting off, much as the bear had done in the old days, and they cared for Bubber in the same way they had cared for the bear, watching to see that he didn't spill things or burn himself; and when he came back from his other world, he'd tell them stories of places he'd been to and what he'd seen there—sometimes halfway across the the universe and sometimes just a few feet away. He began to know things without any reason to know them. He found Russell for them, and he told them joyfully of his progress. How despite every conceivable hardship he was alive and well, and heading for the bear like an arrow. Slowly and painfully, to be sure, but with his lion blazing like the sun. He told them of their brothers, the crows. The guardians. Who, having no faith in their own goodness, still worshipped the lion with all their heart, and fearlessly protected those whose fiery manes were beginning to bud and flower. And the bear! The bear lived! Not just as a lion, but as the bear! The fat, hulking, beautiful bear they loved so much was still among them, and would return before they knew it. Marion and Ida smiled and nodded at this news as they did with everything he said, and to keep himself free from their impossible sorrow, Bubber took to talking less and humming more. Sometimes Ida and Marion joined him, and when they did it together, flashes of light jumped between them and made them one, and Ida and Marion were stronger afterward. They didn't know why, or care, but it didn't matter either. Their lions would stand more proudly than before, and blaze brighter, so they did it often.

Then one day the ache began. A longing for something undefinable. No matter what activity Bubber engaged in it nagged at him, and made him so melancholy that he finally begged for the bear to come and tell him what to do. He found himself returning to the cave repeatedly, where he would feel the bear's presence most strongly, and one night, without any fear or guilt, he went inside and sat quietly in the dark, waiting and hoping for some answer to his emptiness, and the bear came to him. "What's wrong with me?" he asked the bear. "Why do I ache so? There's a hole in me where the light leaks out. What's missing? What is it that I'm doing wrong?"

"Something has not yet been completed."

"Can you tell me what it is?" asked Bubber.

"Look inside," said the bear.

Bubber focused tightly on the bear, and in a clouded picture he saw a vision from his own distant past. He watched as millions of lemmings leaped into the ocean to drown themselves. He watched himself try to join them. He watched as he stumbled at the last minute and fell into a crevice that saved his life, and he watched the sun come up on the day that followed. He listened to his young self make silent resolves about his destiny, and he watched himself walk away from the death place without looking back. He saw the heads of young survivors peek out of their burrows.

"Where are you going?" they called out.

"I don't know," Bubber answered.

"Help us here. There's a lot to do."

"No," Bubber called out.

"You have to help," one called out to him. "We all have to help each other."

"*You* help each other," Bubber said. "I'm not one of you."

"Yes, you are!" they shouted. "You are a lemming. You are one of us."

"Not any more," said Bubber. "I'm not a lemming any more."

"What are you then?" they called.

"I'll let you know when I find out," said Bubber. He pointed himself true east and went on his way.

The image faded, and the lemming who was a lion turned back to the bear who was a lion.

"Is it clear now?" asked the bear who was a lion.

"It's the hole in me," said Bubber, "there's no question about that. I ache now more than ever."

"You made a promise," said the bear who was a lion.

"So I did," said the lemming who was a lion. "What must I do?"

"Keep as much of it as you can stand," said the bear who was a lion, knowing how painful it would be. "Keep it till the light stops leaking out of you."

"Must I go back among them? Back to stay?" asked the lemming who was a lion.

"Just tell them," said the bear who was a lion. "Tell them what you now know. Tell them what you have become. Tell them what they are. That was the promise you made."

"Will they listen?"

"Of course not. Did you listen? It is the nature of

lemmings to destroy themselves. It is their destiny and their desire. You will infuriate some of them, you will be laughed at by the rest; but still, you made a promise. And who knows? Maybe some among them will listen. A few who trust the truth in your eyes. One or two who can clearly see your lion. Perhaps you will even find one who without one word knows fully what you are and never leaves your side."

The lemming thought long about the bear's words and knew without question that it was what he must do.

"It's a difficult task," he said.

"Yes," said the bear who was a lion. "but not impossible."

"Did you know it would end this way?" asked Bubber. "Did you see it like this from where you sit now?"

"No," said the bear who was a lion. "I hoped for it, but I could not have known it. You could have willed some other path. It could have been some other way."

The lemming who was a lion looked outside the cave and saw that the sky was as clear as it had been in weeks, and he took it as a sign. "If I am to go, this might be the time," he said.

"Yes, go," said the bear who was a lion. "I will be with you."

"And I with you," said the lemming who was a lion. He left the cave and the ache was gone.

CHAPTER 23

With Bubber gone, Marion went about the business of living, but she was closed up and shut down. She did her work mechanically, devoting herself only to the moment-to-moment tasks that confronted her. Her feelings were dead. There was no joy in her, no hope, just a plodding instinct to survive, and for what purpose she didn't know or care. Bubber's protestations that he would be back soon, that his place was at the clearing had no effect on her. She heard him, but the news didn't go in anywhere. She had no more room. She had stopped thinking, or planning or caring. The pain in her had been converted to steel, and so she devoted herself to nothing but the routine maintenance of the clearing, and minimal care for Ida. If she had been able to think, she would have truly expected things to continue this way forever, but she had stopped thinking. Then one morning, out of the mist hobbled something that was perhaps once a bird. There was bare skin showing through in patches all over his body, and where feathers remained, they were broken and threadbare. He held a crutch under one wing to hold him upright, one foot was twisted up into itself, a piece of its beak had been broken off, and it whistled when it breathed. Marion recognized him immediately.

"Gareth?" she said as if in a dream. "Is that you, Gareth?"

"Marion? Is that Marion? Is it Marion?" said the creature as it hobbled up to her to get a better look.

"Oh my," said Marion, her voice quivering with all the subtle emotions that she had sworn were dead in her. "Oh my, Gareth," she said touching him gently. "Oh my dear lovely Gareth, look what they've done to you." She caressed his broken face and nestled into him and held him, and he her, and she kissed him on all his wounds and broken places.

"I knew I'd find you, Marion," her Gareth said. "I never stopped looking, you know. In all these years, Marion, not one day went by when I didn't search for you, and look what's happened. Look what's happened, Marion."

"Shhh, Gareth, shh now," she said, holding him and patting him and in her touch bringing him back to life, and herself along with him. She traced the lines of his face and found her old familiar beautiful Gareth underneath all the scars and missing pieces, and the two parts were one thing, and in spite of all her promises and vows and hopes, she was happy once again.

And in the midst of her awakening joy an owl flew into the clearing. It flapped around awkwardly from tree to tree eyeing the inhabitants with a confused look. "Where am I?" he called out. "What place is this? Is there a duck here?"

"Yes, I'm a duck," Marion answered.

"Is there a lemming here? A possum?"

"There is, yes."

"I have a message for you."

"What is it?"

"I can't remember. Something about a bear."

Marion's heart skipped a beat. "What about a bear?"

"Give me a minute, here," the owl said. He landed on a branch and scratched his head with a huge claw. "Somebody described this place to me, you see, then I forgot about it but when I flew over, I said, 'Say, this is that place!' It opened up the memory banks."

"What was the message from the bear?" Marion asked desperately.

"Yes. From the bear." The owl looked at her blankly. "A message from the bear. Or possibly about the bear. Or maybe both."

"Was it a big white bear?" Marion asked, not daring to hope. "Can you remember that much?"

"A big white bear. I think it was."

"What about him?" Marion was practically shouting now.

"Hold on a second. It's beginning to piece together." The furrow in the owl's brow was causing his eyes to pop almost out of their sockets.

"What about the big white bear!" Marion shrieked.

"Hold your horses," said the owl, "it was a while back, and I have other things to think about. This isn't the only thing in my life."

"Tell me about the bear!" Marion screamed.

"Oh yes!" said the owl, striking his forehead. "I remember now. It's a message *from* the bear. It's definitely a message *from* the bear."

"Did you see him?" shouted Marion, "Did you actually see him?"

"I did. Yes. It's all coming back to me now. Large fellow. White. Soft-spoken. I met him on an ice floe."

"An ice floe?"

"Yes. With a couple of seals."

"Seals?" called Marion.

"Yes. Small ones. Babies. They *looked* like seals anyway, but one was painted blue and the other red, so I don't want to be held to that."

"Yes? Yes?"

"We talked for a while. . . . "

"What did he say?"

"He asked me which way I was headed."

"Yes? And then?" Marion said, unable to contain herself.

"I told him I was coming in this general direction, which I ultimately didn't. That's what caused the memory flap, you see."

"The message!" Marion shouted. "What was the message!"

"Ah yes!" said the owl. He struck himself on the head again. "The message from the bear. Let me try to get it right now." His eyes rolled up and he stared intently into his own head. "Yes!" he said, snapping back into focus. "Here it comes, now! He's on the ice floe!"

"Is that the message?" Marion called, half crazy with impatience. "Is the message that he's on an ice floe? Is that it?"

"Yes it is."

"What else? Is there more?"

"Yes!" said the owl, excitedly. "I've got it now! He's on the ice floe, and he'll be back as soon as there's a thaw! Yes. That's it. That's the message." He nodded happily to himself and began to fly off.

"Oh please, please wait!" Marion called to him. "Come down and tell us everything!"

"I can't!" called the owl. "I'm late enough as it is. This took me very far out of my way!" He flew off and Marion watched him fly as if he were her own soaring heart. It was too much. Too much. It was all being returned to her and she knew with these gifts that she had really never stopped believing. That, as bottled up and choked as it had become, it had never gone away. She looked at her beloved Gareth and the joy was so great in her she thought she might burst. She began dancing around the clearing with her wings spread wide.

"What is it, Marion?" Gareth said to her, hobbling after her, sharing in her excitement without a clue as to what it was all about. "What's happening?"

She laughed and swept him up in her dance, too elated to explain anything to him. "*Everything* is happening, Gareth!" She held him out for inspection and twirled him around and around.

"What is it Marion? What's so exciting?"

- 185 -

"I can't tell you, Gareth, you'll think I'm crazy," she said, and she knew then, she really knew, past all of her beliefs and feelings and hopes and needs and fears and cares that they were indeed lions.